To Mandy – challenge accepted!

SOMEONE ELSE'S HONEYMOON

PHOEBE MACLEOD

Boldwood

First published in Great Britain in 2022 by Boldwood Books Ltd.

Copyright © Phoebe MacLeod, 2022

Cover Design by Leah Jacobs-Gordon

Cover Photography: Shutterstock

The moral right of Phoebe MacLeod to be identified as the author of this work has been asserted in accordance with the Copyright, Designs and Patents Act 1988.

Every effort has been made to obtain the necessary permissions with reference to copyright material, both illustrative and quoted. We apologise for any omissions in this respect and will be pleased to make the appropriate acknowledgements in any future edition.

A CIP catalogue record for this book is available from the British Library.

Paperback ISBN 978-1-80426-244-3

Large Print ISBN 978-1-80426-240-5

Hardback ISBN 978-1-80426-239-9

Ebook ISBN 978-1-80426-237-5

Kindle ISBN 978-1-80426-238-2

Audio CD ISBN 978-1-80426-245-0

MP3 CD ISBN 978-1-80426-242-9

Digital audio download ISBN 978-1-80426-236-8

Boldwood Books Ltd

23 Bowerdean Street

London SW6 3TN

www.boldwoodbooks.com

1

A toothbrush. That's what finally unravelled just over ten years of Josh and me. A fucking toothbrush – can you believe it?

* * *

Josh and I have been together since sixth form. He joined from another school after his GCSEs and, although we had a few classes together, I have to confess I didn't really notice him. I was going out with Darren Childs at the time – he was one of the most popular boys in our year and I was punching above my weight there for sure. This is how it works: popular boys go out with popular girls, less popular boys with less popular girls and so on all the way down the ladder to the undateables at the bottom. Darren was in the top league, being both extremely good-looking and good at sports. All the girls had a crush on him. Although I was popular and had a good circle of friends, I was minor league compared to him.

Darren and I were in the same classes for a number of subjects for our GCSEs, and were made to sit together and work together a lot. Needless to say, there were a few raised eyebrows when he started going out with me, but we just clicked somehow, and I loved the extra kudos that came with being his girlfriend. He was also the boy to whom I lost my virginity, as part of the celebrations after he captained our football team in an inter-school match that we won 5–0. I can't remember much about the sex now, apart from it being uncomfortable and mercifully brief, but it didn't do my social standing any harm once word leaked out that we'd 'done it'.

Unfortunately, it turned out that Darren wasn't immune to the charms of other girls, and when I discovered him getting a blow job from Jennifer Adams behind the Science block a month or two into the Lower Sixth, I lost it. I screamed, shouted, and I think I even threw some stuff before storming off around the corner and bumping, literally, straight into Josh. Just as I was stumbling out an apology and trying to help him pick up the books that I'd knocked out of his arms, Darren came running around the corner after me, with Jennifer sauntering along behind him. Darren looked mortified, but I'll never forget the look of satisfaction on Jennifer's face. She knew she'd split us up, and she didn't care how low she'd had to stoop (literally) to do it. I didn't speak to Darren again, and Jennifer later got pregnant after an apparent mishap with a condom and had to drop out of school, so maybe there is some justice in the universe after all.

Josh was brilliant. He took me to a local coffee shop, bought me a hot chocolate and a pastry, and let me pour out my feelings. We missed a whole afternoon of school and ended up in detention together, but from that point on we were firm friends and, after a while, boyfriend and girlfriend. We both went to Bristol University – me to study Dental Hygiene and him Economics. Josh's parents bought him a flat in Tunbridge Wells after we graduated, and it seemed only natural that we would move in together. We've lived here for six years and, until Josh started his latest job, we were pretty happy.

Josh is an only child and his parents dote on him – hence the flat. He's never really wanted for anything and, as a result, was pretty laid-back about finding work after he graduated. My career path was pretty straightforward: after graduating I got a job as a dental hygienist at the Fairoak Dental Practice in Speldhurst, and I've been there ever since. Josh drifted in and out of a few things before he started working at a company called Earthkind a year or so ago. Earthkind specialises in eco-friendly products – you name it, they have an eco-friendly version of it, and Josh has thrown himself wholeheartedly into it. Having been a solid 'meat and two veg' man for as long as I've known him, Josh is now vegan, believes that 'Big Pharma' is trying to poison us, and that most consumer goods are killing the planet. The irony that his flat is paid for out of his Dad's earnings at GlaxoSmithKline is completely lost on him.

To begin with, I was pleased that he'd found something that energised him, and I tried to be supportive and embrace the changes he wanted to make to our lifestyle. However, more recently, it's started to put a strain on our relationship. Don't get me wrong, I'm all for saving the planet, but I'm not a beans and pulses kind of girl and I don't think I can ever be. Josh has also taken to being very critical and holier-than-thou if I don't embrace a particular change. For example, I've always used disposable razors to shave. Last year, Josh declared them to be an environmental disaster and suggested I should embrace the 'natural me' and let the hair grow. When I made it very clear there was no way that was going to happen, he brought home a safety razor ('The blades are recyclable, Charley'). Have you ever tried to use one of those things? After a couple of literal bloodbaths, where I cut my legs and armpits to ribbons, I reinstated the disposables, which I now have to keep hidden in the bathroom cabinet because Josh says they offend him.

Back to the toothbrush.

Ever since we moved into the flat, Christmas has pretty much followed the same formula. We wake up early, open our presents to each other, have languid Christmas sex and then go to my parents' house for lunch. On Boxing Day, we go to his parents. This year I've spent a small fortune on a hoodie he wanted from the Earthkind range, made of organic cotton and recycled plastic bottles. It's not the sort of thing I would choose, but it's worth it to see his face light up as he opens the eco-friendly wrapping paper that costs twice as much as the normal stuff.

And now it's my turn. With a flourish, he produces a small, lumpy-looking parcel. 'Ta-dah!' he exclaims. 'Go on, open it.'

Straight away I can tell that this is not the Miss Dior perfume that I'd had my eye on, or even the new pair of trainers I'd been dropping heavy hints about, but deep down I've always known that he'd never buy me either of them. I unwrap the parcel to find an ugly-looking toothbrush made out of some sort of wood, and a tube of tablets that claim to be the new eco-friendly toothpaste.

'Umm, Josh. Why have you bought me a toothbrush?' I'm struggling to hide my disappointment and hoping desperately that this is just a joke present, that the proper present is going to be revealed at any moment. One look at his face is enough to disabuse me of that hope though.

'It's great isn't it, Charley?' he enthuses. 'It's made from bamboo and the bristles are made from plant-based ingredients so they're biodegradable. I've got you a year-long subscription so a replacement will arrive automatically when this one wears out. Same with the toothpaste tablets. No more tubes of toothpaste going to landfill. One in the eye for Procter & Gamble, eh?'

'Josh, I don't want to sound ungrateful, but why on earth would I want a bamboo toothbrush? I've got an electric one, and what sort of person gives their girlfriend a toothbrush for Christmas anyway?'

'But, Charley, this is so much better for the environment than your electric one. No batteries, no plastic, and it's not just the one – as I said, I got you a whole year's subscription.' He's looking a bit miffed now but, as I realise this is my actual present, I'm far too pissed off with him to care. I can feel the resentments of the last few months bubbling up to tip me over the edge, and before I know it, I'm letting rip.

'Josh, I DON'T WANT A BLOODY BAMBOO TOOTH-BRUSH!' I yell. 'I also don't want whatever these tablets are. I have a toothbrush, and toothpaste. I'm a sodding dental hygienist – I think I know what's best for my teeth!'

He looks genuinely confused. 'I thought you'd like it. Scarlett suggested that, if you liked it, you might spread the word...'

'SCARLETT?? So you didn't even choose this shitty

present yourself, but instead just blindly bought something your colleague suggested for a bit of free marketing? You didn't even stop to think whether it might be something I actually want?'

'Doesn't the planet matter to you? I thought we were in this together.' He's still not getting it.

'Of course it does, Josh! But, if you want people to switch to eco-friendly products, you've got to make them at least as good as the alternative and, ignoring the fact that this is the shittest Christmas present ever, this bloody toothbrush isn't even close. I've tried my best with all this Earthkind stuff, I really have, but take the deodorant that you keep bringing home. It feels horrible and I don't think it works. I've had to resort to keeping a Sure roll-on in my bag and use that instead. I don't like the Earthkind lipstick either – it smells and tastes weird, and it doesn't go on properly. Do you remember the mooncup you forced on me because tampons are bad for the environment? What a fucking disaster that was! Thankfully I had a spare set of scrubs so I could get changed before anyone else noticed that I'd bled all over them, and I've never used it since.

'You just assumed I would go vegan with you because it was what you decided to do, but you never asked me, Josh, did you? I don't even like most of the food you cook, but you've never noticed because you're too caught up in your own world!'

'Charley,' he's getting defensive now, 'you *know* how important this stuff is to me. You *agreed*—'

'No, Josh, I never AGREED to anything because you never ASKED. Instead I've had to try to make things work for me without upsetting you and your beliefs and, frankly, it's getting very hard to do.'

I'm not done. 'You expected me to come off the pill because you didn't like us being at the mercy of pharmaceutical companies, like the one your dad works for, but you wouldn't use condoms either for the same reason. You expected me to take my temperature every bloody day to work out when I was fertile because I haven't got enough to do. Well guess what – I'm still on the pill. How could you expect me to entrust my contraception to a massively convoluted system that seems unreliable to me, when there is a simple and effective solution available? For God's sake, Josh. When did you stop thinking about me in all of this?'

There's an awkward silence when I finish. I can hear my breathing, ragged from pouring out my pent-up frustration. I feel a sense of relief at having got some of it into the open, but I can tell that something fundamental has shifted, and not in a good way.

At last he speaks. 'I give up. It seems whatever I do these days makes you unhappy. It feels like we spend all our time arguing. We didn't used to argue like this, did we? Maybe we need a break from each other, a bit of time to figure out whether we still want to be together.'

'What? What do you mean?'

'I think you should move out for a while, to give us a bit of perspective.'

'Where the hell has this come from? You can't just go from "Here, Charley, Happy Christmas" to "Oh, can you move out please?" in ten minutes flat.'

He sighs. 'You're right. I've been thinking about it for a

while. I'm evidently not making you happy, I haven't been that happy either recently, and I just feel we need time apart to reflect on whether this is just a phase, or whether we've run our course.'

'Is that really how you feel?'

'It is, sorry.'

'And you decide to drop this when we're about to go and celebrate Christmas with my family? How is that supposed to work? What am I supposed to tell them?'

'I think it would be better if I didn't come to your parents today, don't you? Tell them something came up. I'll do the same tomorrow. I'm going to go for a walk now, give you a bit of space to calm down. You take whatever you need, and send my best to your mum and dad.'

This is all moving way too fast for me to keep up with. 'And how long is this "break" going to be? Are we talking a couple of days, a couple of weeks, a couple of *months*?'

'I don't know. As long as it takes, I guess. Let's talk when we're ready.'

He grabs some clothes and shuts himself in the bathroom. A few minutes later I hear him leave, closing the door quietly behind him. I can't believe how calmly he's just ripped the rug from under my feet. It may be his flat legally, but it's my home just as much as it is his. And it's so frustratingly typical of how he is these days; he didn't even pause to check what I thought, just imposed his will and expected me to comply.

After Josh leaves, I sit motionless for a while, trying to process what has just happened. It felt like every other Christmas when I woke up this morning, but in no time at all everything has changed. What does this 'break' actually mean? Is he using it as a cowardly way of finishing with me without actually saying the words, or does he just need time to process what I've said and come to terms with it? Maybe he's right, and some time apart will help us to get some perspective. This has all come completely out of the blue though, and I feel numb with shock.

Eventually, I force myself into action. The first problem is deciding how much to take. All the furniture and stuff in the flat belongs to Josh, naturally, but there are a few things we've added together over the years. If I take everything I want now, then it just makes it feel final. If I don't take everything, and the separation drags on or we split up for good, then I might have to ask him if I can come and collect the rest, which will doubtless be another awkward conversation. As I stand under the shower, I decide that I'll take all of my clothes, but leave everything else so he's not totally rid of me.

The next issue is where on earth am I supposed to go? I've lived here for six years, and it's not as if I have my own flat that I can just move into. I know I can stay at Mum and Dad's tonight, but I have no idea where to go after that. I'm in a daze as I get dressed and start packing. We don't own any suitcases, because suitcases are for normal people who go on nice holidays, so I'm forced to make do with whatever I can find. In the end I fill four bin bags with clothes and load them into my battered old Nissan Micra ('Much better to keep this one running than buy a new car, Charley. Do you know how much energy it takes to build a car?').

As I reach under the bed to start collecting my shoes, my hand lands on a piece of fabric. Our flat has never been particularly tidy, and there are all sorts of things under the bed I'm sure, but as I pull it into the light I can see that it's a pair of knickers. They're blue, thong-type things with lacy details on the front panel.

They aren't mine.

I know this because my knickers are all bog-standard cotton bikinis that come in multipacks. Josh has always said that sexy underwear doesn't do it for him and, on the very rare occasion I've worn anything like the knickers now in my hand, I've found them scratchy and uncomfortable. Also – I check the label – these are a size eight and I'm a size twelve.

So, if they're not mine, whose are they and what are they doing under our bed?

A nasty suspicion begins to creep in. Josh has been talking about Scarlett a lot recently, about how passionate she is, and how much he admires her work. A couple of weeks ago I actually joked to him that perhaps he should marry her because they sounded perfect for each other. He got very defensive and said she was just a work colleague that he admired on a professional level. Now I can't help wondering whether he's been admiring her on a personal level too. I can't leave until I know for sure. I put the knickers on the table in the kitchen and finish loading my stuff into the car. Once everything is packed and loaded, I sit down to wait for him.

When I hear his key in the lock, my resolve briefly begins to crumple, but I don't have an escape route now, so I'll have to go through with it. As Josh walks through to the kitchen and sees me sitting at the table with the knickers I see his eyes widen for a moment before his composure returns.

'I thought you would have left by now. What are those?'

'You tell me, Josh. I found them under our bed. Whose are they?'

'Well, if they were under the bed, they must be yours. I'm not a secret cross-dresser if that's what you think.'

'Are you serious? When have you ever seen me in a pair of knickers like this? You need to do a lot better than that. I'll ask you again: whose are they?'

He looks at me blankly for what seems like an age, and then his shoulders sag. 'I can explain. I'm going to make a cup of tea. Do you want one?'

'No, thank you. I'll wait until I'm at Mum and Dad's and have a proper cup of tea. The stuff you bring home tastes like wet sawdust.' Now that I've started saying what I really think about the Earthkind products, I don't seem to be able to stop.

He opens his mouth as if to protest, but clearly thinks better of it. Instead, he busies himself with boiling the kettle and faffing about with the teabag. Once he's done, he sits down opposite me.

'Well?'

He sighs, and I know what's coming next. It hits me like a punch in the gut but, strangely, I don't feel the urge to cry.

'Are they Scarlett's?'

His eyes widen as if I've slapped him. He stares at me for a good few seconds, obviously trying to decide whether to tell the truth or not, before answering.

'Yes, I think they must be.'

'What do you mean, you think they must be? How many other women have been undressing in our bedroom?'

'OK. Yes, they're Scarlett's.'

'In our bed???'

'It was just the one time here, OK? She came over unexpectedly one Saturday morning when you were at work and...'

'How very convenient that she should choose to drop in unannounced when you knew I wouldn't be here. An almost unbelievable coincidence, in fact. Tell me, is she in the habit of leaving her knickers in other people's houses, or is this a one-off message for me?'

'What do you mean?'

'Oh, come off it, Josh! Do you really think she would have left them here by accident? Any woman in her right mind is going to notice pretty quickly that her knickers are missing when she gets dressed. She *wanted* me to find them, you idiot. She's probably been going mad with frustration that it's taken me so long. So, tell me how long this thing between the two of you has been going on.'

I swear I don't recognise my voice. It sounds disembodied, like someone else has hijacked it. Every fibre of me is tense though, and my heart is thumping like it's trying to escape through my ribcage. I feel sick.

'About two months. Look, Charley, it really was just the one time here. I didn't mean it to happen, honestly.'

'Give the boy a round of applause for being considerate enough to shag her elsewhere! What was it, a clichéd hook-up in the stationery cupboard at work every so often? A little contortion in the loos? I know, maybe you liked to book yourselves into hotels as Mr and Mrs Smith. I hope you found some that charge by the hour; I'd hate for you to be paying for a whole night when you're probably only in there for ten minutes. How can you honestly say you didn't mean it to happen? Were you just innocently loitering around with your dick out when she accidentally fell on it? Don't treat me like a fucking imbecile. How did it start?'

He sighs. 'Like I said, you and I have been arguing a lot recently, and Scarlett and I have been working very closely together on some projects, and things kind of grew from there.'

I know exactly what grew and it makes me want to castrate him.

'Were you planning to man up and tell me at any point, or were you just hoping to keep me and Scarlett as some sort of harem?'

Another sigh. 'I don't know. Scarlett kept saying I should tell you, but it never seemed to be the right time.'

'Well, your timing couldn't be much more perfect now, could it? Merry Christmas, bastard.'

'Charley, I'm really sorry. I never wanted to hurt you...'

'Oh, spare me the bullshit, Josh.'

And with that, I get up, place my keys on the table and walk out of the flat, banging the door behind me.

2

The tears start as soon as I close the car door. Big, fat and salty, they cascade down my cheeks until I'm a snivelling wreck. Snot is running down into my mouth as I take huge gulps of air between sobs. I can't believe what has just happened. It's taken just over two hours for the last ten years of my life to fall apart. I'm suddenly single, homeless, and everything I own (which isn't much) is crammed into this crappy car. I don't even own decent bags to put my stuff in – I'm a bag lady. The thought makes me laugh hysterically for a moment before the misery comes crashing back in. What on earth am I going to do?

Josh has been cheating on me with Scarlett. Now that I know the truth, I just can't get my head around it. Yes, we've had a bit of a sexual dry patch lately, but I thought that was because he was tired after working late so often. Well, he's been working late all right, just not in the way that I thought. An image crashes into my mind of them kissing, of him touching her like he touched me, and I feel sick again. No, actually, I really feel sick. Hurriedly, I open the car door and retch into the gutter. I keep retching until there's literally nothing left and I'm dry heaving.

'Are you OK?' An elderly man and his wife are standing on the pavement looking at me with a mixture of concern and horror on their faces.

'Yes, yes, fine – sorry. I'm just a little under the weather.'

'Are you sure you should be driving? I don't want to pry, but if you had a heavy night last night...'

They think I'm hung-over! If only I were – if only that was all that was wrong with me. At least the vomiting has stopped the tears for now.

'Don't worry – I think it's a stomach bug. I've been feeling a bit off colour for a couple of days.' I have no idea where the lie came from, but I'm just desperate for them to leave me alone. I feel so humiliated, I want to crawl into a dark corner and never come out.

'Well, it's your decision, but it looks to me as if you shouldn't be driving anywhere. You want to be tucked up in bed until you feel better.'

I think of our bed upstairs in Josh's flat. I'd love to go back and undo the last two hours. To be tucked up in bed and start this day all over again. To have a different story unfold – one that doesn't involve my boyfriend sleeping with his work colleague. I need to get out of here.

'Don't worry, I'm feeling much better now. I'll be fine.'

I smile at them, close the car door and start the engine. Immediately, Whitney Houston starts crooning about how she will always love me. Hastily, I eject the cassette (yes, my car is old enough to have a cassette player), pull it out of the player and hurl it into the back of the car. Over the years, Josh has delighted in finding compilation cassettes in charity shops for us to play in the car. I'm tempted to throw the lot of them out of the window, but I'm conscious that the elderly couple are still standing there, watching me.

As I prepare to pull out of the parking space, I glance automatically in the mirror. Fuck. Who the hell is that? The face staring back at me looks nothing like me. My eyes are red and puffy. My cheeks are shining where the tears have been running down them and there are tracks where my make-up has run. There's also a nasty river of snot between my nose and my top lip. I reach into the glovebox for a tissue to wipe away the worst of the damage, and then I set off for my parents' house.

As I drive, I realise that I need to do something about my face. If I pitch up looking like I do now, I'll terrify my nieces and face a full-scale interrogation from my mum, and I'm not sure I'm strong enough for that right now. On any other day I'd stop at a supermarket and avail myself of their loo to fix myself up, but it's Christmas Day and they're all shut. After a few miles I see a garage and, joy of joys, it's open. I pull onto the forecourt, stick ten pounds' worth of fuel into the Micra (well, it's rude to use their facilities and not buy *anything*, isn't it?), and dash into the grimy loo clutching my bag. What is it about garage loos, especially unisex ones? If I wasn't desperate, the smell alone would drive me away, and that's before we get to the suspicious wet patches on the floor with bits of loo roll floating in them. I take a piece of clean loo roll from the holder and use it to turn on the tap; I don't want to touch anything in here if I don't have to. After carefully splashing some water on my face, patting it dry with yet more loo roll and redoing my make-up, I'm starting to look slightly more human, even if I still feel terrible. My toothbrush is deep in one of the bags in the car, so I grab a bottle of water and some extra strong mints on my way to the till. Hopefully between them they'll get rid of the lingering taste of vomit in my mouth.

My parents live in Sevenoaks, in one of those houses where you need a code to open the gate. Dad is what they call a 'self-made man'; he worked for several years as a long-distance lorry driver before starting his own haulage business some twenty years ago. Over the years he's built it up and he now has over fifty trucks in the fleet. In the early days my mum worked with him as his administrator/assistant/dogsbody but when the business took off she 'retired', and for the last few years her life has revolved around her home, her friends, and her various yoga classes. As I pull onto the drive the front door opens and there stand my two nieces, Grace and Bella. They aren't twins but they may as well be; Grace is seven and Bella is one year younger. As soon as I shut off the engine and open the door, they charge across to me, yelling 'Auntie Lottie!!!' I'm barely out of the car before they've entwined themselves around me.

'Girls, let your auntie get inside at least before you mob her! Hi, Lots.' My brother, Simon, strides out of the house. He's five years older than me, but the gap seems much bigger. He's married, with his two gorgeous daughters, has his own house and works for my dad. Dad's grooming him to take over when he retires.

The girls retreat into the house and he gives me a hug.

'How are you? Can I carry anything?' He peers inside the car and exclaims, 'Jesus, Lots, are you *living* in here?'

'It's a long story that I don't want to get into right now, Si. The presents are in the boot – hang on.'

As I fiddle with the boot – there's a trick to opening it – I can see Simon trying to work something out.

'Does the story have anything to do with the fact that Josh doesn't appear to be here?'

'Just leave it, please, Si. How's Emma?'

The opportunity to talk about his wife and family proves just the distraction I hoped it would. 'Oh, she's on good form, thanks. Talking about getting a puppy, would you believe? As if the girls aren't enough to cope with!'

He smiles indulgently and I hand him the bag of presents to carry in and place under the tree. The boot creaks ominously as I close it.

'This car really is knackered, Lots. It's practically held together by the rust. Are you sure you can't afford a new one?'

This is an argument Josh and I have had several times recently, and I've always lost it as Josh has overruled me with his facts and figures about the wastefulness of new cars. If he were here, he'd wade in and give Simon the lecture, but as he's not I just smile and shrug. The car is the least of my worries right now.

My parents' house looks like it's come straight out of one of those homes and interiors magazines. All the walls are painted in muted shades of creams and greys, and there are tasteful pictures and knick-knacks dotted about. As I walk into the living room, I spot the girls lying on the carpet, glued to some cartoon on the television, the excitement of my arrival already a thing of the past. My dad is in his favourite chair just behind them, a glass of champagne already in his hand. He leaps up to hug me.

'Charlotte, Happy Christmas! Lovely to see you – how was the drive over?'

'Hi, Dad. Happy Christmas!' My parents are the only people who call me by my full name. Everyone else abbreviates it in some way. My dad is a big man and I feel a little bit like I'm trying to wrap my arms round one of those Pilates balls when I hug him, but he's a gentle giant and, when he squeezes me in his embrace, I usually feel that nothing can hurt me as long as he's around. I can sense him looking over my shoulder, searching for Josh.

'Where's the weirdo?'

'Josh wasn't able to make it. Something came up at the last minute. He sends his apologies – sorry, Dad.'

He releases me from the bear hug and smiles at me. 'Shame, I was looking forward to a repeat of his lecture on how my lorries are killing the dolphins. Has he worked out how his lentils, or whatever that shit is that you both eat, gets to the shops yet?'

As you can imagine, since Josh has worked at Earthkind and embraced his new eco-friendly lifestyle, his relationship with my parents has gone sharply downhill. They tolerate him fairly good-naturedly for my sake, but they make no bones about the fact that they think most of what he says is nonsense.

'Mind your language in front of the children, John! Hello, darling, how are you?' Mum walks into the room from the kitchen. She's the opposite of my dad. Where he is tall and rotund, she is small and delicate. I can feel her bones as I hug her.

'Happy Christmas, Mum.'

'Happy Christmas! So, no Josh? That's a shame. I got some of that vegan nut-roast thing you both like. Still, extra helpings for you, eh? John, get Charlotte a drink – she looks parched.'

She takes in my face. Although it's a lot better since my impromptu garage stop, it's obviously still a bit puffy and, if anyone is going to notice, it's my mum.

'Are you OK, love? You look like you've been crying. You two haven't had a bust-up, have you?'

I can feel the tears bubbling up again and swallow hard to suppress them. I'm determined not to spoil Christmas for my family by sobbing all over the place.

'I'm fine, Mum, don't worry. Josh just had something that he had to deal with urgently. He sends his apologies.'

'It had better be life-threateningly urgent to make him abandon his girlfriend on Christmas Day,' Dad remarks as he hands me a glass of champagne.

'The important thing is that you're here,' Mum says. 'Come through into the kitchen and say hello to Emma when you're ready. She's been helping with the turkey – some new Nigella recipe she found on the internet, apparently.'

I take the glass from my dad and follow Mum into the kitchen, just as Emma is taking an enormous turkey out of the Aga.

'I'll baste it now, Christine, and then it should be ready to rest in another thirty minutes. Hello, Lots, Happy Christmas. I'd hug you but I've got my hands full right now.'

'Happy Christmas, Emma. That turkey looks amazing.'

'Thanks. It's a recipe that your mum agreed we could try.'

I've heard countless tales of friction between mothers and daughters-in-law, but my mother and Emma have got on famously ever since Simon first brought her home, years ago. They even went on holiday together every year for a while, but that had to stop when the girls started school. Mum and Dad did invite Josh and me last year, to be fair, but Josh would rather have ripped his own eyes out than set foot on an aeroplane, so I politely declined.

'Simon tells me you're thinking of getting a puppy?'

'Well, the girls have been going on and on about it and, as I'm not working, I thought a dog might be nice company while they're at school and Simon's at work. We're trying to decide between a Labradoodle and a Cockapoo. We're visiting a couple of breeders early in the New Year.'

'I suggested they might want a dog that didn't shed,' Mum adds, 'so Emma doesn't have to spend all her life hoovering up fur. Also, it will make less mess here if we end up having it to stay.'

I smile. 'I might have known you'd be in cahoots with this!'

At that point Simon joins us in the kitchen. 'Are we nearly ready to open presents now Lots is here? The girls have finished their cartoon and are getting antsy.'

Emma shoves the newly basted turkey back into the oven, where it's joined by a big tray of roast potatoes that my mum has prepared.

'Yes, we'll just take our aprons off and top up our glasses. Get the girls to start organising the presents into piles.'

As we walk back into the living room a few minutes later, Grace and Bella are industriously taking presents from under the tree, looking at the labels, and adding them to the growing piles at various stations round the room.

'Auntie Lottie, you're over there,' Bella tells me, pointing at one end of the squishy leather sofa under the window. 'Mum, you're between me and Grace on the other sofa, with Dad on the end. Nan, you and Grandad are on the same sofa as Auntie Lottie.'

We all take our places and the ritual of present opening begins. The girls go first, squealing with delight as each new item is unwrapped. Emma and Simon are trying to keep track of what they've received and from whom, so they can say their thank-yous later, but it's a challenge.

Once Bella and Grace have finished, the rest of us take turns to open our presents. Before long, the living room looks like a storm has passed through it, with piles of opened presents, discarded wrapping paper and ribbons everywhere. Amazingly, there isn't a ridiculous bamboo toothbrush to be seen anywhere. I still have no idea how Josh thought that was an acceptable present.

Emma and my mother disappear back into the kitchen to finish preparing the Christmas dinner.

'Well, I think we've all done very well,' Dad declares. 'Let's get this lot cleared up and have a little top-up before we get called through.'

As we bundle the used wrapping paper into a bin bag, I can't help noticing a solitary present left under the tree. 'You can take that and give it to Josh, Charlotte. Your mother chose it. It's nothing big – he's not the easiest person to buy for, she says!' Dad's eyes twinkle mischievously as he says this.

'Umm, yeah, OK.' I have no idea what I'm going to do with it, but I don't want to think about it now. One thing at a time.

Before long, we're called through to the dining room, where the table is groaning under the turkey, trimmings and vegetables. Mum has obviously been in and rearranged it since I arrived, as there is no awkward empty space where Josh should have been sitting. I give her a grateful smile as I sit down. After we've all admired the turkey, Dad sets about it with his carving knife. He did a course a few years back, and now he takes great pride in knowing how to carve pretty much any joint of meat. Emma busies herself sorting the girls out, while my mum passes plates to the rest of us.

'How big a piece of this nut roast would you like, Charlotte?'

'Actually, Mum, would you mind very much if I had turkey instead?' It looks so good, and my stomach practically growled with anticipation when I spotted the pigs-in-blankets.

If she's surprised, she hides it well, and passes me a plate of turkey without a word. I add potatoes, vegetables, pigs-in-blankets, gravy and bread sauce. I can sense my family watching me, but I don't care right now. If I'm really single again, and the evidence of this morning would indicate that I am, then I can eat whatever I like, can't I?

It all tastes as good as it looks, and my empty stomach rumbles in appreciation as I eat. Thankfully, the conversation round the table is loud enough that nobody else hears. I gladly accept a second helping as the food and wine start to numb the ache in my gut. Normally I limit myself to one glass as I have to drive home, but I have no home to go to this year so I allow my glass to be topped up.

After two helpings of Mum's Christmas pudding and a glass of port to wash them down, I'm full. The girls have skipped off to play with their presents some more, Dad and Simon are deeply engaged in a conversation about something to do with the business, and Mum and Emma are talking dogs. Every so often Mum looks at me quizzically, as if she's trying to work out what's going on, and I know that she hasn't bought a word of my story.

3

'Charlotte, would you mind very much helping me to clear the table and load the dishwasher?'

Here we go. She may be a small woman, my mum, but she takes no prisoners. As the others file into the living room to let their Christmas dinner go down, Mum and I start to clear the table and stack the plates in the dishwasher. She deliberately lets the silence settle between us; I know exactly what she wants to ask, but she's waiting for me to tell her in my own time. I busy myself with washing up some of the glasses that can't go in the machine, so I don't have to look at her as I speak.

'Josh and I have been having a few difficulties. We've decided to spend some time apart. Is it all right if I stay here for a few days?' As the words leave my mouth the tears start to flow again. I lower my head as if I'm concentrating on the sink so my mother can't see.

'Oh, love... I knew something was up. What happened?' She comes up behind me and wraps her arms around me, resting her head between my shoulders. This simple act of kindness tips me over the edge, and the tears start falling much faster. I turn around and we hug tightly.

'He's been seeing someone else behind my back, Mum. Someone from work. I think it's over. I just don't know what to do!' The words are now punctuated by sobs as I dissolve into a soggy mess once again. So much for not spoiling anyone's Christmas.

She says nothing, just holds me and lets me cry. After a while, I notice the shoulder of her dress has a dark damp patch on it from my tears.

'I'm ruining your dress!' I exclaim as I gently break out of the hug.

I can see her switch into practical mode. 'Oh, don't worry about that. Let's focus on you. Of course you can stay here for as long as you want. Your father will probably be pleased to have someone other than me to talk to. You can go into your old room. I was going to put the girls in there tonight, but we can set them up with sleeping bags on the floor somewhere. They'll think it's a great adventure. You stay in here until you feel ready and leave everything else to me. Do you want me to ask Simon to bring your stuff in from the car?'

I think of the bin bags full of clothes stuffed into the Micra, and Simon's reaction when he saw them earlier. 'No, it's fine, Mum. I'll do it later.'

'OK, I'll leave you now and go and sort the others out. Come through when you want to.'

As I continue washing up the glasses, I listen to the murmur of conversation in the living room as Mum fills the rest of the family in on my situation. At one point I hear Dad's voice clearly as he says, 'Has she given the weirdo the heave-ho then? Do we need more champagne?' followed by my mother obviously telling him off.

Emma pops her head around the kitchen door. 'I'm just going to move the girls' stuff. I'm so sorry to hear about you and Josh. If there's anything we can do...'

'Thanks, Emma, I think I just need a bit of time to come to terms with it at the moment. Sorry to muck up your plans.'

'Don't be ridiculous. The girls are delighted. They're already working out where best to put the sleeping bags so Simon and I don't tread on them when we go to bed. Really, don't worry about it at all. Give me five minutes and the room will be all ready for you.'

She's lovely, Emma. I can see why Simon married her. Temperamentally she's not that different from my mother; she's generally pretty chilled, but on the rare occasions I've seen her riled, she's been terrifying. She loves her girls to bits, but they don't get away with anything. The puppy, if they get one, will be a model of obedience, I'm sure.

I finish tidying the remains of the meal. The leftovers all go into the fridge in plastic tubs, the way I know Mum likes them. I pop a tablet into the dishwasher, start it, and wipe down all the surfaces. Something about performing these menial tasks is soothing, and I start to feel a bit better. Once I'm done, the kitchen is spotless. Time to bring my stuff in from the car.

As I push open the door of my old bedroom with the first bin bag, I take a moment to look around. I know lots of parents keep their children's rooms as some sort of shrine to their adolescence after they leave home, with the posters on the walls and everything, but my mother has never been sentimental like that. Instead of the single bed I slept in when I was growing up, there is now a generously sized double, and the walls have been repainted in a restful shade of green. The contrasting cream curtains have a floral pattern on them that picks up the colour of the walls, and the carpet is cream coloured to match the curtains. Everything is colour-coordinated, down to the green duvet cover on the bed. The white flat-pack wardrobe and desk that I covered in stickers and boy-band posters have gone, replaced by a sturdy-looking pine wardrobe, a chest of drawers and a dressing table with a mirror. There are bedside lights on either side of the bed, throwing a soft light across the room. It's a weird mix of familiarity (the shape of the room, its location in the house and the view from the window), and the totally new. I don't think I've actually set foot in here since I moved out to live with Josh. We've visited regularly, of course, but only ever for the day, so I can't remember the last time I came upstairs in Mum and Dad's house. I dump the bag on the floor and go back downstairs to fetch the next. Once everything is in from the car, I sit down on the bed and try to summon up the energy to start unpacking it all.

* * *

I'm awoken by the sound of the girls thumping up the stairs to have their bath. Glancing at my watch I realise that I've been asleep for two hours. Deciding that the bin bags can wait, I check my appearance in the mirror. Not great. My hair is all frizzy where I've been lying on it. I dig out my hairbrush and brush it until it looks semi-passable before putting it back into my trademark ponytail and going downstairs. As I walk into the room and glance at the tree, I notice that the single present underneath has disappeared. Good old Mum.

'Ah, there you are!' Dad exclaims as I walk into the living room. 'Did you have a good sleep? Your mum came to check on you and you were completely sparko,' he adds with a chuckle.

'I've put cheese and biscuits out in the dining room, with some sliced ham and other bits and pieces. You know how it works, love, just help yourself when you're hungry.' My mum is sitting in the chair next to Dad, flicking through the TV schedules on her iPad. 'There doesn't seem to be anything on that we want to watch. There's the *Call the Midwife* Christmas special, but that will probably send your father to sleep. Is there anything particular you'd like, Charlotte?'

'No, I'm fine.' Josh and I have normally headed off home by this point on Christmas Day, but the routine hasn't changed since I was little, so I know what to expect and the rest of the evening passes very pleasantly. People help themselves from the spread in the dining room as and when they want to, Grace and Bella pass through giving everyone sloppy goodnight kisses before Emma puts them to bed, and nobody asks me any awkward questions. I drink a couple of glasses of wine and join in the general conversation, but by ten o'clock I can feel my eyelids drooping, so I make my excuses and head to bed.

* * *

* * *

Once I've dried myself and got dressed, I wander down to the kitchen in search of breakfast. Mum is in there, leafing through a home improvement magazine and sipping from a mug of coffee.

'Morning, Charlotte, did you sleep well? You look loads better this morning.'

'Thanks, Mum, that bed is really comfortable.'

'Good. Help yourself to whatever you like for breakfast. There's cereal, bread for toasting, eggs, you name it. I think there's even some smoked salmon left if you fancy smoked salmon and scrambled eggs. I'm assuming you're eating things like eggs and fish again after yesterday?'

'Yes. To be honest, Mum, I was never a very good vegan. My love for bacon sandwiches kept derailing me.' I smile at her.

As I busy myself with choosing cereal and getting the milk from the fridge, she fills me in on her plan for the day.

'Emma, Simon and the girls are going to head off mid-morning, and your father has gone to play golf, so it's just you and me today. I'm going to go to the garden centre this afternoon with Judy and see if I can bag a bargain or two in the sale. You're welcome to come with us if you like.'

'Thanks, Mum, but I probably ought to sort out my clothes and unpack.' I need to start restoring some sense of order to my life and, although I like her, Mum's friend Judy doesn't have any tact at all. An afternoon of her quizzing me about my love life is the last thing I need right now.

'OK. The offer stands if you change your mind though.'

Once they've all gone and I'm alone, I make a start on unpacking. As I do so, I try to make a plan. I can't think beyond the next few days at the moment, but that's enough for now. At some point I expect I'm going to have to talk to Josh again. I wonder if he's tried to get hold of me. I fish my ancient iPhone out of my bag and switch it on. The battery life is so poor now that I keep it turned off unless I'm actually using it. No missed calls and no texts. I wonder what he's doing. Is he going to his parents' house with Scarlett? I'd like to be a fly on the wall for that one. I've always got on extremely well with Josh's parents and I think they rather hoped we might marry one day. Fat chance of that now. As I feel the sadness welling up again, I make a positive effort to push thoughts of Josh and his family from my mind and focus on the task in hand instead, but a few tears fall anyway.

God, I have some ugly clothes. I've never really thought much about it before, but in these plush surroundings some of my stuff looks incredibly tired and dilapidated. Shapeless tops, baggy jeans, tired sports bras, and the less said about some of my knickers the better. I hold a pair up to the light. I remember them being a rather pretty shade of pink when I bought them. Now they're more grey, and they're fraying where the elastic meets the fabric. The contrast between these and the ones I found under the bed couldn't be more marked. I bet Scarlett wouldn't be seen dead in knickers like these. The fabric itself is so worn it's practically translucent. I tug it between my fingers and it tears easily. I decide to make two piles. One pile for clothes that still have life in them, and another for those that have definitely passed their use-by date.

By the time I've emptied the bin bags the 'throw away' pile is significantly larger than the 'keep' pile. I bundle the 'throw away' pile back into the black bags to take to the recycling and put away the rest. Thankfully, I don't actually need that many clothes. I wear scrubs at work, and it's not as if my diary is jam-packed with social engagements over the next few weeks. Even after binning more than half of them I reckon I still have just about enough clothes to be going along with for now.

By the time my parents are back, I'm fully unpacked and I've made a trip to the recycling bank to drop off the bin bags of worn-out clothes. I feel a sense of achievement, but I'm very conscious that there are another six days to fill before I go back to work on the second of January and pick up some semblance of my normal life. I plug the iPhone in to keep it charged and sit cross-legged on the floor by the plug to call my friend, Madison.

I met Madison the day I moved in with Josh. She lives in the flat opposite ours and we hit it off straight away. Although she was born in America to American parents (hence the name), her accent is mostly pure cut-glass British – a legacy of the expensive private education her parents put her through after they moved to the UK when she was small. I've never met her father; he works for some big international corporation and travels a lot, but her mother has been at the flat a few times when I've popped over. It's bizarre listening to them chat; Madison's accent reverts to a broad American twang when she's talking to her mother, but switches to British the moment she addresses me.

She works as a freelance journalist, so she's often at home during the day. I got into the habit of popping over to hers for a decent cup of tea and a chat whenever she was around on my Wednesday afternoons off, and we've become firm friends.

She picks up almost instantly. After the usual 'How are yous?' I fill her in on the situation between Josh and me.

'Oh, Charley, I'm so sorry. What a bastard! I'd offer to fire-bomb his flat for you, but it might burn mine down too.'

When I tell her about the trip to the recycling bank, she squeals with delight. 'But you see what this means, Charley, don't you? You've just thrown away half your wardrobe and the post-Christmas sales are on. You and I are going to hit Blue-water and get you a whole new look.'

'Mads, I'm not sure I'm up to a big shopping trip right now.'

'Nonsense. Best thing for you. After I'm done with you, you'll feel like a new woman!'

'I don't think I want a new woman. Last time I looked I was still very much heterosexual.'

'Ha ha. I see your break-up hasn't improved your sense of humour. I'm at Mum and Dad's until tomorrow. I guess you won't want to come over to mine in case you bump into Josh and whatshername, so I'll pick you up from your parents the day after tomorrow. Bring credit cards.'

We agree a pick-up time and she rings off.

I'm not sure I'm ready to reinvent myself yet, but once Mads gets the bit between her teeth there's no deflecting her. I guess it will fill a day even if I don't buy anything, and she's promised to pay for lunch, so what's the harm?

4

Mads picks me up as arranged, and we arrive at Bluewater just after it opens at ten. My suggestion of a coffee before we start is dismissed.

'No time, too much to do.' Mads starts dragging me through the shopping centre. When we arrive at our first destination, I'm surprised to see we're standing outside a lingerie store.

'Now, we're starting from the inside out. There's no point getting you lots of lovely new stuff if you're wearing crappy underwear underneath. Tell me, when was the last time you bought a new bra?'

'Umm, I don't know.'

'And what sort of bras do you like – wired or not wired? Push-up? Balcony?'

'I normally just buy sports bras to be honest. They're good for work.'

'Honestly, Charley, you're hopeless! Sports bras are fine for keeping everything in place if you're exercising, but there are so many different types and they all do different things for you. That's why you need expert advice and that's why we're here. You're going to have a bra fitting.'

'What?? I don't need a bra fitting! I know what size I am and, anyway, they look busy. We'll probably have to wait for ages. Let's start somewhere else.'

I daren't confess that I've never had a bra fitting. My mother tried to persuade me to have one when I was a teenager, but I managed to dodge her by just trying on loads of different sizes until I found one that I thought felt right. It's a technique that's worked just fine for me ever since.

Before I can object any more, she pulls me inside, marches up to the counter and says to the assistant, 'This is Charlotte Jenkins. She has an appointment at ten fifteen for a bra fitting?'

While the assistant consults the appointment book, I pull her aside. 'You booked me in?'

'Oh yes, as soon as they reopened yesterday. Trust me, you'll thank me later.'

'Right now, I want to smack you one!'

Before I can carry out my threat, a pretty woman with a tape measure hanging round her neck comes up to us and asks, 'Which one of you is Charlotte?' Mads practically thrusts me at her.

'I'm Tina,' she says, 'and I'll be doing your fitting today.' She leads me to a changing room at the back of the store. I guess she's in her late thirties, but she has one of those faces that make it very difficult to tell. She could be older and just ageing well. I'm so wrapped up with trying to work it out that I miss the fact she's speaking to me.

'Sorry?'

'I said we won't be disturbed in here.' She draws the curtain closed and I find myself in a large cubicle with a full-length mirror in front of me. Oh joy. In my experience there's nothing quite so unforgiving as a full-length mirror. As well as my own reflection, I can see Tina standing behind me, looking expectant. An uncomfortable silence descends. My skin is prickling. Why doesn't she just get on with it? After what feels like an age, she speaks again.

'So, if you could just slip off your top and your bra, I'll get you measured.'

'What?'

'Your top and bra. If you could just slip them off. There's a stool there you can pop them on.'

She's got to be having a laugh. Does she seriously think I'm just going to whip my boobs out in front of a complete stranger?

'Umm, is that really necessary? I'm sure I read somewhere that you were supposed to be able to tell by just looking at me or something.'

'Charlotte,' she says soothingly, 'I may be good at my job, but I can't measure you by telepathy. There's nothing to be ashamed of. I'm sure you're not hiding anything under there that I haven't seen before.'

I feel cornered. I'd love to make a run for it, but Tina is standing between me and freedom and I don't want to flatten her in my bid to escape. I try to tell myself to be rational, that lots of women get fitted every day, but that doesn't help. It's not even that I'm ashamed of my boobs particularly – they're all right, I guess. It's just, well, embarrassing to think about stripping off in front of someone I've never met, in a shop.

'Would you like me to step outside while you get undressed?' Tina is asking now.

How on earth would that help? I wonder. That's like asking if I'd like her to count to ten before she chops my head off. The result is the same, it's just drawing the process out. I grit my teeth and resolve to murder Madison as soon as we're alone and I can think of somewhere to hide her body.

'No, it's fine.' Reluctantly, I lift my jumper over my head, and then reach round to undo my bra. I dump them on the stool and stand there staring fixedly at the floor, my cheeks burning.

'Excellent. So, what I'm going to do is measure round your ribcage, just under your bust. That will tell me your underband size.' She gently wraps the tape measure around me and notes the measurement. 'Now I'm going to measure round your bust, and the difference between the two will tell me your cup size. Once I've done that and we know what size you are, I'll go and get some bras for you to try. OK?' Once more the tape goes around.

'Right, Charlotte. You're a 34C. Stay there and I'll be back in a minute.'

I open my mouth to ask her if she's sure she has measured me right, because I'm pretty certain I'm a 36B, but she's already gone. I hear Mads' voice from the other side of the curtain.

'How are you getting on?'

'Seriously, Mads? I'm plotting your demise in here.'

'Relax. The worst is over. Now comes the good bit.'

Tina reappears with her arms full of bras. 'We'll start with this one. It's a T-shirt bra. It'll give you a nice shape under close-fitting tops.' She hands me the bra and I put it on. At least I'm partly covered up now. She fusses with the straps for a few moments and then says, 'There you go. What do you think of that?'

I force myself to look in the mirror and my first thought is *WHOA! Where did THEY come from??* Once I'm over the initial shock, I have to admit to myself that I like what I'm seeing. My normal sports bras tend to just squash and minimise, but this is really flattering. I can't help smiling as I turn left and right, admiring my new décolletage. Tina then makes me try on various different styles, including a push-up bra (would madam like to wear her boobs as earrings, or use them to poke people's eyes out?), and a plunge bra, which is supposed to enhance your cleavage but just makes me giggle hysterically. In the end I buy two T-shirt bras in different colours, with knickers to match. After I've paid for them, Mads insists that I go back into the changing room to put one of the sets on before we go and look at anything else.

'You may have been right about this, but I still want to kill you,' I tell her as we leave the store.

'Rubbish, you should thank me for rescuing your poor tits from years of wrongful imprisonment!'

I laugh and glance downwards. It's like two aliens have taken up residence on my chest, but I can't help smiling (34C – did I mention that?).

'OK, Mads, where next?'

'Wait and see.'

It turns out that our next port of call is a mobile phone shop. This has the potential to be every bit as traumatic as the bra fitting, but for different reasons. I know that my iPhone is on its last legs and I did go into a shop to see about replacing it a few months ago, but I was so confused by all the different options and technical jargon that I ended up thanking them politely and, not to put too fine a point on it, fleeing with my tail between my legs.

Once again Mads takes charge, but this time I'm grateful. It's almost like she's acting as a translator between the sales guy and me.

'What sort of contract is your current phone on?' she asks me after several minutes of incomprehensible conversation between her and the sales guy.

'Umm, it's pay-as-you-go.'

'OK, what about data? How much do you use?'

'I don't. I wasn't sure what I'd use it for or how much it would cost, so Josh showed me how to turn it off.'

Mads rolls her eyes in despair. 'OK, let's start her with this package. Is that OK price-wise for you, Charley?' She points to a contract costing £45 per month. It includes '4GB of data', whatever that is.

It's a lot more than my pay-as-you-go has been costing me and Mads obviously senses my reluctance. 'The new iPhone only costs £50 if you take this one, so it's not as bad as it looks,' she explains.

It seems like we've been in the store for an age by the time we finally emerge. I thought the forms would never end; the phone company practically knows more about me than I do. However, the sales guy has transferred my contacts onto the new phone for me, and set it up so I can get my email on it as well. Thankfully, Mads decides it's now time for lunch, and we set off for the restaurant.

Once we're settled at a table and we've placed our orders, she commandeers my new phone.

'I'm bringing you into the twenty-first century,' she tells me. 'I'm installing Spotify and WhatsApp for starters, and then we'll get onto your social media.'

'I'm not a total dinosaur, you know! I've used WhatsApp – we have a group for work. I'm not sure Spotify is going to be much use though. Where am I going to listen to it? You've seen my car, right?'

'Well, it won't do any harm. Right, what social media are you on?'

'I've got a Facebook account, but I haven't looked at it in ages.'

'OK, we'll start there.' She starts downloading the app just as the first course arrives. It's a mixture of different types of mezze and it's delicious. As soon as we've wiped the plate clean with our bread she's back onto my phone.

'It's installed. OK, what are your login details?'

'I think the account is my email – cjenkins1042@ yahoo.com – but I'm not sure I can remember the password.' I try to cast my mind back. 'Try Josh4Me4Eva.'

'Classy!' Mads sniggers as she enters the details. 'Yup, we're in. Wow, look at this! When did you say you last looked at it?'

'Oh, I don't know, last year sometime. Josh wasn't a fan of social media.'

She puts down my phone and studies me for a moment. 'Why am I not surprised? I'd love to know how he thinks Facebook is killing the planet. Actually, scrub that. I wouldn't. I've been amazed at how you put up with him lately. Am I allowed to say that?'

'You want to talk to my dad. He feels much the same.'

'He has been getting progressively stranger, you've got to admit. I mean, I wasn't entirely sure what you saw in him when you first moved in, but since he's started on the eco-warrior gig, he's gone full-on wacko. You do see that, don't you?'

'Yes, it was getting a bit out of control. Tell me something, have you ever come across a mooncup?'

'Oh, dear Lord.' She snorts with laughter. 'He didn't!'

'He did. It was a disaster.'

'Was there any aspect of your life he didn't try to control? I mean, surely a woman should be allowed to have her monthly cycle without her boyfriend barging in and mansplaining all over it?'

'There weren't many things he didn't have an opinion on.'

'So it would seem! Anyway, you've got some friend requests.' She hands me the phone. Sure enough, there are requests from some of my old school friends, plus a couple of people I knew at university. I accept them all, and I'm surprised how good it makes me feel that these people have been looking for me online. I resolve to do a bit of sleuthing of my own later.

Once we're finished and waiting for the bill, I summon the courage to ask the question that's been on the tip of my tongue since this morning.

'So, have you seen him?'

'Give me a chance! I only got home last night, and I came out first thing today to collect you. But I did have a little listen at his door on the way out. He's there. I could hear him moving about, and... are you sure you want to know this?'

'Yes! You can't stop now!'

'He wasn't alone. I could hear him talking to someone, and a woman's voice replying.'

The tears are instant. 'Oh, Charley, I'm sorry,' she says.

'No, thank you for telling me. Although it hurts like hell, it's bringing some sort of closure I guess.'

Mads moves round so she's sitting next to me and puts her arm round me. 'You know what? Fuck him. Fuck the bastard.'

Despite the tears, I manage a rueful smile. 'I rather think that's Scarlett's job now, don't you?'

'Well, until he gets bored and cheats on her. Once a cheat, always a cheat.'

'Do you really think so? As far as I know, he was completely faithful until she came along.'

'That may be the case, but he's got a taste for it now, hasn't he? There's no sex so intoxicating as illicit sex, and now he and Scarlett are no longer clandestine, I reckon it won't be long before he goes looking for his next thrill. You're well out of it, I reckon.'

'I wish I could just turn my feelings off and agree with you. I hate him for what he's done, but I also still love him. It's such a mess in my head.'

'Listen, by the time I'm done with you today you're going to be so fabulous and out of his league that he'll be kicking himself every day for the rest of his life for being such a stupid prick. Now, you go and sort yourself out while I pay the bill, and then we'll see what other damage we can do to your bank balance, eh?'

When we finally emerge from Bluewater several hours later, darkness has fallen. If this were a cartoon, my debit card would be sweating and panting from the exertion. The bags of shopping completely fill the boot and quite a lot of the back seat of Mads' car. I've got figure-hugging tops that show off my assets (34C, don't you know), blouses, skinny jeans in a variety of colours, some new ankle-length boots that I'm *very* pleased with, as well as brand-new everyday underwear from M&S. Mads was very resistant to me buying new sports bras, but I pointed out that I didn't want to be unintentionally prodding any of my patients with my breasts while I was treating them so she reluctantly gave in. I did buy a push-up and a plunge bra to experiment with, as the prices were a little less terrifying than the underwear shop, and that pacified her a bit. I've also got a new coat, and a very flattering brown leather jacket that would give Josh kittens.

I had a close shave in John Lewis, where Mads was all for subjecting me to an in-store makeover. Thankfully the makeover stations were all busy, so I managed to dodge that one.

'Have you ever considered doing something different with your hair?' she asks as she starts the car and begins to reverse out of the space.

'Like what? What's wrong with my ponytail?'

'Well, I'm just wondering what you'd look like with it shorter, and maybe some highlights...'

'Whoa, slow down there! There's only so much change a girl can take in a single day.'

'OK, fair enough. Think about it though?'

When we get home and bring everything in from the car, my dad watches us with amazement.

'Good grief!' he exclaims. 'Did you two buy the whole shopping centre?' My mum, meanwhile, is already in my room, taking the clothes out and laying them on the bed, experimenting with different combinations. I swear I hear her sighing with pleasure.

'Haven't you both done well!' she says. 'I bet you look fabulous in this stuff, Charlotte.'

'I had better look fabulous, given what I've spent!' I retort.

'Christine, what do you think about Charley doing something different with her hair?' Mads asks my mum.

'For God's sake, Mads! Don't you ever let up? I said I'd think about it!' I try to push her out of the room in feigned annoyance. In reality, I'm so delighted with my haul that she could probably suggest I shaved all my hair off and I'd listen to her right now.

'She has got a point though, love,' Mum says. 'You've worn your hair like that for as long as I can remember and, while I'm sure it's practical, I'm not convinced it's making the most of your face.'

'Will you two stop ganging up on me? Isn't there somewhere you both need to be? Go on, shove off, the pair of you, so I can change. I'll give you a little fashion show if you're good.'

'OK, I'll leave it for now,' Mads says, 'as long as you let me put my stylist's number into your phone. He's called Paul. Ring him when you're ready and tell him you know me. Promise?'

'Yeah, whatever.' I hand over my phone. 'Just as long as it shuts you up!'

She grins and starts typing.

The rest of the evening is great fun. I try on a few outfits and parade them past my audience in the living room. Even my dad, who is totally uninterested in female fashion as a rule, agrees that I look good, and Mads causes a lot of hilarity by wolf-whistling when I come down wearing the plunge bra under a low-cut top. It's all very flattering and does my battered self-esteem no end of good. Mads stays for dinner and, when I fall into bed later that night after she's gone, I find I'm smiling.

Yup, definitely progress.

5

One of the good things about living with Josh for the last six years is that it's been extremely cheap. He has no mortgage or rent to pay, so he never expected me to pay any rent either. My only outgoings, in terms of living expenses, have been my contribution to the utility and food bills. This means that I'm sitting on a substantial pot of savings, which is going to come in handy as I need to find somewhere to live. Don't get me wrong, it's nice having my meals cooked for me and I'm enjoying Mum and Dad's company, but I'm not a teenager any more and I need my own space at some point.

The first decision is where to look. Sevenoaks is too expensive and, ideally, I'd like to be a bit closer to work. Tunbridge Wells is a possibility. It's a big place and, as long as I'm not too close to where Josh lives or works, I shouldn't bump into him. The other option is Tonbridge, between the two. It's not a town I know particularly well, but it's closer to work than Sevenoaks, and also reasonably close to Mum and Dad if I want to pop in from time to time.

I suspect the lettings agencies will all be closed between Christmas and New Year, but I decide to try anyway, just on the off chance. Black Cat Letting agency is the first one in the Yell.com listing, so I start there. The phone is answered after a couple of rings.

'Black Cat Lettings, Dave speaking. How may I help?'

'Oh hello, I wasn't sure whether you would be open,' I say.

'We're open all right. It's a busy time of year for us. Lots of people looking to move after Christmas to get away from people they suddenly realise they can't stand,' he chuckles. 'Anyway, what can I do for you?'

I explain my situation and that I'm ideally looking for a furnished, one-bed flat with parking in Tonbridge or Tunbridge Wells.

'Furnished is going to be a bit tricky,' Dave explains. 'Most of our lets are unfurnished. It's a lot simpler for the landlord because there's less argument about what constitutes acceptable wear and tear, and of course most tenants have their own furniture that they want to bring with them.'

'Yeah, unfortunately I don't own any furniture at present. I can buy some if necessary, but I was hoping just to move in somewhere for now, while I get myself sorted.'

Dave hums and haws for a bit, as he looks through his listings. I hear him muttering 'No, no, no' as he scrolls, and my optimism starts to fade. 'Ah, here's a possibility,' he says after a bit. 'Do you have to move immediately, or can you wait a little while?'

'That depends what you mean by "a little while", Dave,' I reply.

'Well, let me tell you about the property. It's a one-bed

apartment overlooking the river in Tonbridge. It's just come in and it's a furnished let. The owner has got a work contract in Australia and is moving out there for a minimum of six months, but probably longer. It's got its own allocated parking space and it's on for £800 per calendar month. The only issue is that the owner isn't going away until February so, by the time we've done our inventory and deep clean, you'd be looking at the end of February as a realistic moving date. Is that going to be a problem?'

'I'm not sure. Ideally, I'd want to move earlier if I can. It does sound exactly what I'm looking for, but can you just check whether there's anything else first?'

'Absolutely, no worries. Bear with me and I'll have a look. I'm going to put you on hold so I can consult with my colleague to see if he knows if anything else is coming on as well.'

As the music plays, I consider my options. I could look at an unfurnished flat, but then I'd have to buy all the furniture, which would then take time to come. I'd have to try to organise furniture deliveries around work, and it all sounds quite a faff. I'm sure Mum and Dad wouldn't mind me staying for a couple of months more – after all, they said I could stay for as long as I liked, and I'm sure they meant it.

My thoughts are interrupted by Dave. 'Right, I've looked through and had a chat with my colleague. If you're definite about one bed and furnished, this is the only one we've got at the moment. We do have a three-bed furnished house available, but obviously that's considerably more expensive. We've also got two unfurnished one-bed flats if you're interested. I'll be honest with you though – neither of them are as nice as this one. I'd be happy to show you them if you like.'

'Can you set me up a viewing of the furnished flat please? The timing isn't ideal, but I might be able to make it work.'

'Absolutely, no worries.' This is obviously Dave's catchphrase. 'I hope you don't mind but, while you were on hold, I took the liberty of calling the owner. I can show you the apartment at three this afternoon if you like. I realise that's short notice, but it might not hang around for long so it's probably best to strike while the iron's hot if you can.'

I can spot the sales talk – I wasn't born yesterday. Isn't it odd the way they tell you that anything you want is incredibly desirable and you'll regret it forever if you don't snap it up right away, but if you're trying to sell anything it's always got some serious flaw and they're basically doing you a favour by taking it off your hands? However, it's not as if I have lots of plans for the day and, even if this flat isn't right, it will give me a benchmark.

'That's fine, Dave. I can do that.'

Dave gives me the address and I agree to meet him at the property.

Rather than sitting around at home until it's time to go, I decide to use the time to explore Tonbridge and, in particular, the area around the flat. I'm sure Dave will tell me that it's all very peaceful and very desirable, but I want to form my own impressions.

At first glance, Tonbridge appears a bit shabby and rundown. At the top end of the high street is the boys' boarding school, which looks a little bit like Hogwarts from *Harry Potter*, and at the other end is the train station and a Lidl. In between it seems to be mainly charity shops, vaping shops and discount stores of different types. The high street isn't busy; in fact, the only two places that seem to be conducting a roaring trade are the Wetherspoon's pub and a coffee shop on the corner of one of the arcades. The arcades themselves are mainly deserted, and a lot of the shop units are empty, giving them something of an abandoned air. I'm struggling to see myself living here.

As I explore further, things start to improve. The coffee shop does look inviting, like the sort of place where Mads and I could spend an hour or two happily putting the world to rights, and I discover that there are two decent supermarkets within walking distance of the flat I'm going to see. In fact, Waitrose is literally across the road. My mother will be delighted. Even if there's no way I could afford to do my weekly shop there, it will be a nice place for treats, and there is a decent-sized Sainsbury's about five minutes' walk away, which will do for everyday food. Unsurprisingly, Josh was suspicious of supermarkets; he was sure they were all in cahoots to exploit the suppliers and fix prices, but that didn't stop him using them once he realised the prices in the specialist vegetarian and vegan stores he wanted to use instead were considerably higher.

At three o'clock I walk back to meet Dave. I try to tune out his sales patter as I wander round the flat. It has big windows overlooking the river and is flooded with natural light. The main room has a kitchen area at one end, with a little table and a couple of chairs, and there is a comfortable-looking sofa at the other end with a coffee table in front of it. There's a flat-screen TV mounted on the wall, and Dave informs me that there is a satellite box if I want to take on the subscription. There's even a little balcony that I can imagine myself sitting on with a glass of wine on a summer's evening, watching the river go by. The bedroom is a reasonable size, with a double bed, chest of drawers and a built-in wardrobe. The owner is obviously a man; it has a slightly 'bachelor pad' feel to it, but it's not as spartan and minimalist as it could be. There are splashes of colour here and there, most notably from some abstract art on the walls. It's perfect. I want to move in straight away.

Dave is explaining the letting process. I have to pay a £500 non-refundable deposit to take it off the market. After that they do the standard checks on my income and background to make sure that I'm able to afford it and I'm not going to wreck the place. The rest of the deposit is due once we've agreed the date that I can move in.

On the way out, he shows me the car parking space, which is in an underground garage. Apparently, I'll be given a remote control to open it from the car once I move in. I've never felt particularly vulnerable coming home by myself at night, but I have to admit that I like the extra level of security. I follow Dave back to his office and we complete the paperwork.

'How did the flat viewing go?' Mum asks me as soon as I walk through the door. She's on her own as Dad has had to go into work to sort out an issue with a broken-down truck.

'Well, there's good news and bad news. The good news is that the flat is lovely and I've taken it. The bad news is that I can't move in until the end of February, so you'll be stuck with me until then if that's OK?'

'Of course it is, darling! Your dad and I were just saying this morning how much we're enjoying having you around. In fact, the timing works really well for something that we wanted to ask you. You know how we always go away for a couple of weeks in February?'

My mum and dad are creatures of habit, and their holiday pattern illustrates that. When I was little, and Dad was just starting out with the business, we went to the same static caravan park in Cornwall each year. As the business grew and the money started to flow in, the locations were steadily upgraded. First it was a gîte with a pool in the south of France, and now they go to the same all-inclusive resort in the Caribbean every February and do a Mediterranean cruise every September. Dad always tips over-generously, so that the staff remember him and greet him like a long-lost friend on his next arrival.

'Yes, it's your Antigua trip, isn't it?' I say to Mum. 'Did you want me to watch the house for you while you're gone? I'll be at work during the day, but at least there will be regular comings and goings.' Mum is always worried that the house will be burgled, and they usually pay someone to house-sit when they go away.

'That wasn't what I was going to ask, actually. Your dad rang the travel company to check whether there was still space on the flight and at the resort, and there is, so we wondered if you'd like to come with us? Our treat. We think you could use a break and some sun. What do you think?'

I'm just about to come out with the usual excuses about

why I can't go when I realise that Josh's objections to air travel don't matter any more. I'm a free agent and my carbon footprint, or whatever it is, has nothing to do with him. There's just one thing standing in the way, but I might be able to do something about that.

'Oh my God, Mum, I'd love to! I just have to square it with work.'

'Ah, we didn't think of that.' Her face falls a little. 'Your dad was so hopeful that you'd say yes this time that he's already got the reservations on hold. They only hold them for twenty-four hours though, and your practice doesn't reopen until the second of January, does it? Well, we'll just have to hope there's still availability then.'

'I might be able to get an answer more quickly than that. Leave it with me.'

I fish out my phone and dash off a quick WhatsApp message to Tracey, my practice manager. She's bound to be checking her messages even though we're closed, and she and I have always got on well, so I'm sure she won't mind hearing from me.

Hi Tracey, sorry to bother you on your holidays. Had a bit of boyfriend trouble (long story) and my parents have invited me to go to Antigua with them in Feb. Any chance of time off? Sorry it's short notice. Charley x

I hit 'send', and I see two blue ticks. She's on her phone. Great.

I can see that she's typing a message, and I realise I'm nervous. I'd really like to go on this holiday. The only breaks

I've had in the last few years have been rain-sodden camping trips in various parts of the UK with Josh, so a bit of winter sun would be a real treat. The difficulty is that we have patients booked in for February already, so it creates a bit of administrative hassle for Tracey. At last the reply comes through.

Hi Charley. No problem – was checking work stuff anyway as husband and kids glued to PS4 game. Sorry to hear about boyfriend. Do you need to borrow instruments to hurt him with? Re: Holiday. OMG, of course you must go!!! Don't worry about us, I'll arrange cover once back in the office. Love Tracey x

I show Mum the answer, and we're doing a little victory dance round the kitchen together as Dad comes through the front door.

'I take it you're coming then?' he asks. 'Great stuff. They said they'd try to get us adjacent rooms, so we don't have to spend hours traipsing across the resort looking for each other.'

'Thanks so much, Dad.' I give him a hug and he squeezes me tightly in return. 'My pleasure, love. It's worth it just to see you smile again.'

As I'm getting ready for bed, I realise that there are a couple of things I need to sort out before I can go anywhere. I'm going to need a suitcase for starters. I'm also going to need a swimsuit. I bash out a WhatsApp to Mads.

M&D have invited me to Antigua in Feb. Work says I can go :-D :-D. Where's a good place to buy a swimsuit? Cx

The reply is back in moments.

Brilliant! Just what you need. Not prepared to tell you best place for swimsuit. You will buy something ugly, one-piece, and probably black. You need supervision. Mx

Shit. She's a mind-reader. A black one-piece was exactly what I had in mind.

6

I've done it. I've survived the Christmas break, although New Year's Eve was a little tricky. As I didn't have any other invitations, I agreed to help Mum with the party she and Dad put on every year for a few of the neighbours. I guess it's what would have been called a 'cocktail party' years ago. The guests pitched up at around eight o'clock and I spent the evening passing round drinks and the nibbles that Mum and I had prepared during the day. Dad put the TV on for the countdown to midnight, poured champagne to toast the new year in and then, after a couple of drunken renditions of 'Auld Lang Syne', we pushed them out into the dark to stagger back to their own houses. In the past I've often wondered how they make it home, given how some of them put the booze away, but none of them seem to have fallen in a ditch yet.

I have to say I'm not wild about the neighbours. Frank and Marion, who have lived in 'Fairviews' for as long as anyone can remember, are lovely, but I find most of the rest of them impossibly smug and self-satisfied. George, from 'Shooter's

Lodge', is the worst. I don't think there is an 'ism' that he hasn't embraced. He's racist, sexist and vocally homophobic. His topic of choice this time was 'all these damned migrants trying to cross the Channel so they can ponce off our benefits system. It's not our fault their countries have gone to the dogs. Send them all back, that's what I say. I blame the French. They don't want them so they just encourage them to come here.'

His equally awful wife, Jean, egged him on with remarks like 'George feels very strongly about...' and 'George has written to the *Daily Mail* about...' If she noticed that he openly ogled my chest every time I offered him a drink or a snack, she chose to ignore it. I, on the other hand, wanted to slap him. They might be 34C, George, but they're not for you.

Anyway, it's over, and I'm on my way to work. I've been looking forward to coming back and regaining some sense of normality after the events of the last week but, as I park in my usual spot in the car park, I feel rather discombobulated. Everything looks the same, and yet everything in my life is completely different from when I was last here. I remember wishing everyone a Merry Christmas and Happy New Year as we locked up at lunchtime on Christmas Eve. I was looking forward to getting home and wrapping up the presents I'd bought for Josh and my family while listening to some Christmas songs on the radio, and maybe having a glass of wine or two. Everything was broadly OK in the world, and I was looking forward to spending a few days with my boyfriend and our families. Now, just a week later, all of that is gone.

What am I supposed to say when people ask me how my Christmas was? I'm not worried about the patients – they're not really interested and only ask because it's a way of making conversation. I'll tell them it was fine, as that's the expected response. But I'll have to tell my work colleagues some of the truth, even if I gloss over the worst bits. I also don't want to go over the story countless times with them one by one, as I really don't think I have the strength for that. I could put a sign up in the kitchen I suppose: 'Charley and her boyfriend split on Christmas Day. He was seeing someone else. She's coping as best she can. Be gentle with her please', but that seems a bit clinical.

As I walk through the door, I spot Tracey waiting for me. She calls me straight into her office.

'Happy New Year and welcome back, Charley. How are you?'

'Honestly, Tracey? I've been better, but I think I'm over the worst.'

This isn't strictly true. I'm still prone to bursting into floods of tears. Usually it's either when I'm alone in my room and the reality that Josh and I are no more comes crashing into the forefront of my mind, or when I allow myself to imagine what he and Scarlett are doing at that moment. But it can also be triggered by completely random things, like a particular song on the radio that reminds me of him. Have you ever noticed how many songs are about relationships and break-ups? I hadn't, until Josh and I split. Now, every song seems to be about broken hearts. I've had to install a box of tissues in the car in case of random crying fits. I reckon I'll be OK at work though; we have the radio on in the background to help patients relax, but I don't really hear it as I have to be completely focused on what I'm doing.

Tracey is looking at me with concern. 'Do you want to tell me what happened, or would you rather not?'

I fill her in on the broad brushstrokes. A couple of tears escape and run down my cheeks, but I do feel more in control, being in this environment. She hands me some tissues to wipe them away. When I explain my anxiety about having to repeat the story over and over again to everyone at the practice, she leans forwards.

'Ah well, I've been thinking about that and I have a plan, if you're up for it?'

'Go on.'

'Well, you tell me how much detail you want to share. I'll then give the story to Rachel, but tell her that you don't want anyone to know yet, so she has to keep it to herself. I guarantee you that, by lunchtime, everyone will know and you won't have had to do a thing!'

I can't help but laugh. Rachel is one of our receptionists, and everyone likes her, but we've also all learned, some of us the hard way, that she's completely incapable of keeping a secret. In fact, it's worse than that, because she's not above adding her own little embellishments here and there to make the story sound more interesting.

We agree what Tracey is going to tell Rachel, and then I go off to my treatment room to get ready for the first patient of the day. When I tell people what I do, their normal reaction is something along the lines of 'Oh, I couldn't do that. Poking around in people's mouths – what if they have really bad breath?' but the fact is that I love my job. It's not just scaling and polishing, although that is a large part of what I do. I also talk with patients and give them advice on how to improve their oral hygiene. I keep detailed records and, when a patient comes back and I see an improvement, it's very satisfying. I also really like the team I work with. We're quite a small practice and, despite the fact that we all work in our own rooms, we're quite a tight-knit community.

My morning patients come and go, and I lose myself in the rhythm of my work. Most of them are regulars that I've been treating for a few years, but there are a couple of new faces as well. There are two hygienists in our practice – me and Sue. Sue is quite a bit older than me – her oldest child is only four years younger than me – and I found her a bit overbearing when I first started here, but now we get on extremely well.

The practice is open on Saturday mornings for those patients who really can't manage to get in during the week, so Sue and I alternate on Saturdays. When I'm working on a Saturday I get Wednesday afternoon off instead, but I have to confess the Saturday mornings are my least favourite part of the job. It's not because I'm working when everyone else is having a weekend, it's just that the patients we tend to get on Saturdays are so infuriating. For example, there was one guy who was actually answering emails on his phone while I was trying to do his scale and polish. I had to ask him to stop, as his arms were getting in the way of what I was doing and, from his reaction, you'd have thought the entire City of London was going to grind to a halt because his reply was delayed by twenty minutes. Last time I checked the City was still there, so I think we got away with it.

After the last patient of the morning has left, I make sure everything is ready for the afternoon session before wandering into the kitchen/staffroom to retrieve my lunch from the fridge. Since moving back home I've re-embraced my inner carnivore, and today I've got some sandwiches with leftover beef, horseradish, tomato and rocket.

Rachel has been true to form, and I'm treated to lots of compassionate nods, and the occasional 'Sorry to hear... If there's anything I can do...' type of remark as the dentists and other members of staff file in and fill up the chairs around the edge of the room. Of course, we all know there's nothing any of them can do, but it's nice to feel supported. Carl, who joined us a couple of years ago, offers to perform a full extraction for Josh without anaesthetic, which makes me smile. As usual, I discover Rachel has gone off-piste and told them all that I caught Josh and Scarlett in the act, but I don't have the strength to contradict her. It doesn't really make any difference to the outcome whether I caught them or not.

While I'm eating, I fish out my phone and have a quick scroll through my Facebook feed. Since accepting the friend requests a few days ago I've been looking up some of my other old school friends, as well as a couple of enemies. Quite a few of them are married now, with small children that dominate their posts. One or two are divorced, and Paula, who I used to sit next to on the bus, is on husband number two. Samantha ('Call me Sam') Carter is in a lesbian relationship; I'm sure that's not a surprise to anyone. I manage to find Darren Childs who, according to his profile, is living in Aberdeen. There aren't many details and he's not shared his relationship status. Despite my best efforts, I don't manage to find Jennifer – I try with both her maiden name and his surname but none of the matches are her. I wonder whether she's also in Aberdeen, or if they've split up. Thinking about other people's lives is a welcome distraction from my own. I'm not remotely interested in getting in contact with Darren and won't be sending him a friend request, but I indulge myself in an imaginary conversation with him:

'*So, Darren, how are things with Jennifer?*'

'*Don't mention her. Total bitch. I should never have done what I did to you, Charley. I've regretted that day ever since. You were the best thing that ever happened to me, you know?*'

'*Well, you should have thought of that before sticking your dick in her mouth, shouldn't you? You know the best thing about that day for me? It's that it led me to Josh, who is twice the man you are. He's never...*'

Ah, damn. That didn't go to plan.

Anyway, Facebook has generally been a good addition to my life. Quite a few of my friends are still in the area, and we're trying to plan a meet-up in one of the pubs we used to go to. It's proving more challenging to organise than when we were young, as it's got to be fitted in round jobs and childcare, but it seems from the latest round of messages that next Thursday evening is looking promising. That'll be something to look forward to.

The afternoon follows broadly the same pattern as the morning. I have one new patient who, from the look of his teeth, has managed to live his whole life to date without coming into contact with a toothbrush, bamboo or otherwise. He's seeing the dentist after me, and I think Carl will have to take most of his teeth out (hopefully with anaesthetic), but I do what I can for him. I think we'll be seeing a lot of him over the next few months.

My last patient of the day is Mrs Mills. According to

Rachel, she's a powerhouse of the local community, regularly terrorising both the governors and PTA at the local school, as well as dominating the parish council. As I don't live in the area, I have to take Rachel's word for it, but I find it hard to marry up the forceful woman that she describes with the one that I treat. Put simply, Mrs Mills' Achilles heel is that she's terrified of the dental chair. We always put her last on the schedule so I can spend extra time with her if I need to.

By the time I've coaxed her into my room, checked her medical history and whether she's had any issues since the last appointment, and got her settled in the chair with a bib and protective glasses on, we're already ten minutes into her thirty-minute appointment. I'm always extra careful to explain to her what I'm doing at every stage, to demystify it and reassure her.

'OK, Louise, so first of all I'm going to check your gums. You might feel a bit of pressure from the probe. If it gets uncomfortable in any way just let me know and I'll stop so you can have a minute. All right?'

'Yes. Wait! Is the probe sterile?'

'Yes, Louise. Remember what I told you last time? Everything we use is sterilised in an autoclave, which kills all bacteria. You're quite safe.'

The rest of the appointment follows the same pattern and, by the time she leaves, nearly an hour later, everyone apart from Tracey and me has packed up for the day and left.

'How was it?' Tracey asks me.

'Well, Rachel came up trumps!' I smile at her. 'Carl even offered to take all Josh's teeth out for me. Might have made a pretty necklace I suppose.'

'Nice idea. A little medieval for my tastes, but whatever floats your boat. I've sorted cover for your holiday by the way.'

'Oh brilliant, thanks so much! I haven't been abroad in years, and I can't wait to soak up a bit of sun.'

'You're more than welcome. Do you mind if I make an observation?'

Uh-oh. Where's she going to go with this?

'Go on...'

'Well, I know you and Josh were childhood sweethearts and all, but I couldn't help wondering, the last few months, whether he was actually making you happy. You just seemed, I don't know, a bit like Tigger when he lost his bounce. I know the whole break-up, and him playing away, was shit, but there's a sparkle in your eyes today that I haven't seen for a while.'

'I think you'll probably find that was moisture. There's been a lot of that lately.'

'You're a strong woman, Charley. I know you're going through the mill, but you're a fighter and I reckon you'll be OK. I mean it.'

'Thanks, Tracey.'

She sets the alarm, turns off the lights and locks the door. As I walk to my car in the darkness, I reflect on what she said. I don't feel like a strong woman, and yet here I am functioning reasonably well, albeit with the odd glitch, just nine days after Josh ripped my world apart.

Yeah, maybe I'm tougher than I think.

7

The night out with the girls from school is great fun. Although I haven't seen them for years, it feels as if we're just picking up the conversation where we left off. I'm not drinking because I'm driving, and a few of the others are doing 'Dry January' after overindulging at Christmas, but we're doing just fine without alcohol to loosen the inhibitions. They love bringing me up to date on all the gossip and what everyone is doing now.

I get a bit tearful telling them about Josh, especially as they are all so kind and supportive.

'Would you like me to have him beaten up for you?' asks Samantha ('call me Sam'). We were close friends at school and I feel a bit guilty for letting our friendship slide so easily. She always wore her sexuality like a badge of honour, but the uniform policy and school rules on hair and piercings limited her self-expression. Freed from those constraints, she appears to have embraced every lesbian stereotype available. She's still slight of frame, with an elfin face and large blue eyes, and her hairstyle is the same pixie cut she's had for as long as I've known her, but the impressive array of piercings are new. As well as several in each ear, she has also had her nose, lip and tongue pierced. She's dressed in a white T-shirt with black dungarees over the top, and ankle-length Doc Martens. Also new are the angry-looking tattoos on her bare arms. Despite her diminutive size, I wouldn't mess with her, and I have no doubt that she could make short work of Josh if she needed to.

'That's very kind of you, Sam. I'll bear it in mind.' I smile at her.

After an hour or so, I feel brave enough to ask, 'I couldn't help doing a bit of Facebook stalking the other night, and I see Darren is living in Aberdeen. Is he still with Jennifer?'

'You mean you don't KNOW??' Paula exclaims. 'Oh, this is too good. You're not planning on trying to get back together with him as some sort of rebound thing, are you?'

'No, and what don't I know?' I ask.

'She threw him out four years ago. He was having an affair...'

So far, so Darren.

'... with a man.'

I nearly spit out my drink. 'What? No, you're having me on.'

'Seriously. I don't know what raised Jennifer's suspicions, but apparently she didn't have to grill him too hard before he fessed up. He's moved up to Aberdeen with a guy called Geoff, who works on the oil rigs.'

'Bloody hell, who'd have thought it? I remember how horrible he was to that boy in the year below when he came out. What a hypocrite!'

'You're right, I'd forgotten about that. What was his name – Tom something?'

'Thomas Merriman,' Sam reminds us.

'That's him. I wonder where he is now?'

'Do you think Darren was just fighting against it by going out with you and Jennifer? He could be bisexual, I suppose,' Paula muses.

'Sexuality isn't a binary thing,' Sam begins. This is a well-worn lecture from her, and we can probably all quote it. 'It's a spectrum, and we all sit at different places along it. For example, it's about the person more than the gender for me...'

'Oh, do shut up, Sam!' Paula retorts. 'You've never looked sexually at a man in your life, and you know it!'

Sam laughs. 'Fair point.'

'Bloody hell. Who'd have thought it? Poor Jennifer...' I realise that I'm actually saying that without malice.

'Oh, I wouldn't be too worried about her,' Paula quips. 'Word on the street is she moved someone else in surprisingly quickly, if you get my drift. I'm not sure Darren was the only one up to no good. Now, who wants another drink?'

The conversation drifts through a wide range of topics as the evening wears on. I admire the pictures of their various babies and children, listen to them trying to outdo one another with tales of how useless their various partners are and, before we know it, the landlord is calling last orders. As we go our separate ways, we promise to make this a regular thing. I hope we do. It's been my fault that I've lost contact with them, and I want to make sure it doesn't happen again.

* * *

Thankfully, work has settled down. Everyone was walking on eggshells around me for the first couple of days, but now that they've satisfied themselves that I'm not going to dissolve into hysterics at the slightest provocation, the usual banter has resumed. The practice feels like a welcome haven of stability at the moment, and I'm not even as grumpy as I usually am about working this Saturday morning. Yes, the patients are the usual crowd, and I have to explain to one of them that, no, I can't fit a full scale and polish into ten minutes, but I don't let it get to me. The truth is that I've got other things on my mind, namely the appointment this afternoon.

After my shopping trip with Mads, Mum kept 'casually' dropping hints about booking an appointment with Paul, Mads' hair stylist, so just after New Year I gave in and rang them up. I had to call into his very swanky-looking salon for patch tests during my lunch break a few days ago, and my appointment with him is this afternoon. I'll admit I'm a little bit anxious. I've had the same hairstyle since I was a teenager and I've used the same, slightly shabby, hairdresser down the road from Josh's flat for the last six years. I'm used to a quick wash and cut that takes half an hour, tops. I'm not really a 'salon' person, and I'm slightly worried that Paul will take one look at my ponytail and frogmarch me straight back out of the door. I hope he doesn't, though. I'm ready for a change and, if he is anywhere near as good as Mads claims he is, then I'm happy to go with pretty much whatever he suggests. To be fair, Mads' hair always looks great. It's a beautiful honey-gold colour and falls in loose waves to just below her shoulders. It has that simple elegance that you just know comes with a hefty price tag.

Mads was beyond excited when I told her. 'Oh my God! He's going to make you look so fabulous. What time is the appointment? I want to come and give you moral support.'

'Mads, I'm having a haircut, not a baby! I'll be fine. I'll WhatsApp you a picture once it's done, I promise.'

She's not easily fobbed off, but eventually concedes defeat. I love her to bits, but the idea of her and Paul deciding what's best for me, as if I'm some kind of hairdresser's dummy without opinions of my own, is too much. I don't want a repeat of the bra-fitting ambush. I'm supposed to be an adult, for goodness' sake. I'm sure I can manage this.

As soon as I arrive at the salon, I'm offered a hot drink and Paul guides me over to his chair, where he puts me in a gown. He pulls up a stool next to me, checks the patch test and asks me lots of questions about my current style (if you can call it that) and what I have in mind.

'The only rule is that it either has to be above the shoulder, or I have to be able to tie it back for work. Beyond that I have no idea. I'm open to suggestions,' I explain.

'I can work with that,' he says. 'I've got some ideas of things that we could do, but to narrow it down I'll show you some pictures of different styles that I think would work with your hair, and you can tell me what you like. Is that OK?'

Paul shows me lots of pictures of different hairstyles, and I point out a few. After a while he professes himself satisfied.

'What about colour? Did you want to change it, or stick to the natural colour?'

'I don't know,' I profess. 'I've wondered about going more blonde, but it's difficult to picture, do you know what I mean?'

He nods. 'I think what I'd be inclined to do is just add a

few subtle highlights this time,' he says. 'Your natural colour really suits you, so I think we just want to enhance it and bring it out a bit more, rather than change it, if you're happy with that?'

'Fine with me. You're the expert.'

'Final question,' he says. 'It feels like you're after a completely new look, so would you like to be able to see what I'm doing as I go, or would you rather I covered up the mirror and gave you a big reveal at the end?'

I take a moment to think about it. I'm used to having the mirror there to reassure myself that they're not cutting too much off, so the idea of not being able to see is a bit daunting. On the other hand, I'm not really going to know what it is going to look like until the end, so it might be better to be kept in the dark until then, rather than trying to second-guess what he's doing all the way through.

'I think I'll go for the big reveal, thanks,' I tell him.

He goes off to mix up the colours he wants to apply, and then chats away to me as he and one of his assistants carefully separate strands of my hair and lay them on pieces of tinfoil, before applying paste from one of the pots they have between them, and wrapping them up into parcels. He hasn't covered over the mirror yet, so I watch them as they work. By the time they have finished my head is covered in little silver squares and I look like a pantomime Martian.

'I need to leave that to cook, so to speak. Would you like anything to read while you wait?'

I select a fairly recent version of *Hello!* magazine. It's all the usual fare; some celebrity I've never heard of shows us round her perfect home, someone else has just had a baby, and so on.

It's all gushing prose and beautifully styled pictures. I find myself wondering if anyone actually buys magazines like this, or whether they only ever exist in doctors' waiting rooms and hairdressers'.

After a while the assistant comes back and takes me over to the washing station. The parcels are all carefully removed, and my hair is washed in the most amazing-smelling shampoo and conditioner. I'm also treated to a head massage, which is lovely, but threatens to send me to sleep. When I get back to the chair, the mirror has been covered over.

'Ready?' Paul asks.

'As I'll ever be,' I reply.

He starts cutting. I don't look down to see how much hair is landing on the floor in case I panic and flee. I smile as a mental image of me running down the street comes into my mind. The hairdressing gown is flapping around me, and one half of my head is completely bald. Not a good look.

Paul is very attentive. He asks about work, how I know Mads, and is full of entertaining stories about terrible hair he's had to fix. He's fairly camp, so I'm surprised to learn that he's married, with a teenage daughter.

'She's just started working here on Saturdays,' he tells me. 'At the moment it's just making tea and coffee for customers, and sweeping up, but she's hoping to go to college and train to be a stylist. I think she'll be good. I know I'm bound to say that, being her dad, but she's good with people, and that's a big part of the job. You can be the best stylist in the world technically, but if you can't read your customer and make them feel at ease then you're not going to succeed.'

After what seems like an age, Paul stops cutting. Out comes

the hairdryer and, after a thorough blow-dry, he pronounces himself satisfied.

'Close your eyes,' he commands, and I obey. I can hear the cloth being removed from the mirror.

'Right, when you're ready, open them and have a look.'

It takes me a second or two to summon the courage, but when I do the sight that greets me takes my breath away for a moment. My plain brown ponytail is gone. My hair now ends just below my chin in what Paul describes as a medium bob. The highlights are subtle, but somehow bring a whole extra dimension to the colour. It shines softly from the conditioner, like I'm in one of those shampoo adverts on TV. It's beautiful.

'What do you think?'

I keep swishing my hair from side to side. I can't believe this person in the mirror is me. 'It's amazing, Paul. Really. Thank you so much!'

Paul explains what he's done and shows me how to blow-dry it so it keeps its shape. I make a note to buy a new hairdryer as the £9.99 one I bought years ago in Argos patently isn't going to cut the mustard any more. His bill is fairly eye-watering, particularly once I've added shampoo, conditioner and various masks to keep it looking good, but I pay it happily.

As soon as I'm out on the street I take a selfie and send it to Mads. My phone pings almost immediately with an incoming message.

Told you he was good. You look HOT! <3 <3 <3

8

The hair is a great success. Mum keeps going on about how amazing it looks, and is contemplating booking an appointment with Paul herself. Dad, typically, didn't notice at first and Mum had to prompt him several times. He was very complimentary when he finally worked out what was different though. Even some of the patients at work have remarked on it.

I hadn't realised, until I started this journey of reinvention, how little care I'd been taking over my appearance for the last few years. Josh never seemed to mind what I wore, so I'd tended to gravitate towards comfort over style. My casual 'look', if you can call it that, tended to consist of trackie bottoms, jeans or leggings under a big hoodie top or baggy jumper. I look at myself now, in my fitted top and skinny jeans, with my new hair, and I feel like a different person. There's just one bit of the 'old' me that I haven't addressed yet, and the time has come to do something about it.

'I thought I might go and look at some cars next Wednesday,' I announce to my parents over dinner. 'The Micra really is on its last legs, and I ought to get rid of it before it dies on me.'

'Thank God for that!' my dad replies. 'I'm sure that thing is a death trap. I'll take the afternoon off and come with you if you like. Help you negotiate, make sure you get a good deal. In fact, I could ring John at Mercedes. He might have a nice A-Class or something for you.'

Cars are another area where my parents are very set in their ways. My father dreamed of owning a Mercedes when he was starting out and, as soon as he could afford it, he bought one. Ever since then he's driven nothing else. Now he and Mum both have them – his is some enormous SUV thing, and hers is a sporty convertible.

'Thanks, Dad, but I think a Mercedes is a little out of my price range.' I don't tell him that I also reckon I'm about twenty years too young. 'Don't worry about taking time off work. I'm a big girl now and I reckon I can manage to buy a car unsupervised.'

'Are you sure? Let me at least give you some tips before you go, OK?'

Wednesday comes around, and car-hunting turns out not to be the fun-filled afternoon I'd hoped it would be. Armed with all my father's negotiating tips, such as 'Ask for what you want and then don't speak – force them to make the next move,' and 'Make sure they throw in floor mats for free – ask for those right at the end,' I started the search with high hopes that I'd find the perfect car for me fairly easily.

So far, I haven't seen anything I like, and I've come to realise that the process is complicated somewhat by the fact that I don't really know what I want. I don't want anything too big, but it's got to have something fun about it. I want it to make me smile if I see a reflection of me driving it in a shop window. The tatty Micra makes me look like a student, partly because it dates back to my student days, so I know I want something a bit more 'grown-up' than that. But a lot of the cars I'm being shown make me feel like I should go straight back to Paul and ask for a blue rinse.

The sales people have been awful too. The first guy feigned interest, but I could tell he didn't think I was a serious buyer. He didn't quite say 'Come back with your boyfriend/husband/father' but I could hear him thinking it. He did have one car that I liked the look of, a sporty-looking VW Polo, but when I asked about a test drive, he became very evasive.

'Those are in tremendous demand,' he told me. 'I'd need a pretty firm commitment that you're going to buy it before I could offer a test drive. It's about trust, you see. I don't really know you, so I need to know that you're serious about doing a deal today before we could go any further.'

'I'm not going to commit to buying it before I've even driven it! That's mad!'

'I'm sorry then, miss. I don't think I can help you. It's company policy. Come back and see us when you're ready to buy.' I saw him watching me as I drove off in the Micra; he obviously thought I'd been wasting his time.

The second sales guy seemed to be under the impression that he was my best friend. Vastly overfamiliar, he kept touching my arm and my lower back as he 'guided' me round the various cars he thought might be suitable. He was particularly keen to sell me a Honda Jazz in metallic pink, and kept going on about its merits, even after I told him it wasn't what I was looking for. He also reeked of cheap aftershave and cigarettes and, in the end, I had to make up a forgotten appointment to get away from him.

In order to appease Dad, I did go and see John at Mercedes, but the only car he had that came close to my budget was a bottom of the range A-Class in white, which made me feel a hundred years old as soon as I sat in it. I thanked him politely and fled.

I'm now at the Ford dealership, talking to Grant. So far, he's been professional and courteous, which is a welcome relief after the first two. He's flicking me through the stock list on the screen and, at the moment, it's just more of the same sort of boring stuff that I've seen in the other garages. I'm starting to wonder whether I'll be stuck with the Micra forever.

'Stop. What's that one?' I ask, suddenly.

It's a hatchback in electric blue, with big wheels, a wing on the back and bucket seats. It looks sporty and fun, exactly the sort of car the new me should have. I look at the price and, although it's a bit more than I'd set as my budget, I can still afford it.

'That's a Fiesta ST. It's the sports model of the range. It's, umm, pretty fast. Are you sure?'

Oh, Grant, and you were doing so well up until now too. I smile at him coquettishly. 'What's the matter, Grant? Don't you think I can handle it?'

Suitably chastened, he goes off to find the keys. Half an hour later the test drive is complete and we're back in the showroom. Apart from one slightly hairy moment, when I put my foot down and it took off like a scalded cat (Grant wasn't wrong, it really is fast), the Fiesta and I got on famously. We're now starting the process of 'doing the deal', and Grant is walking me through the finance options.

'Actually, I was planning to pay the whole amount up front and buy the car outright,' I interrupt.

I can see the surprise flicker across his face but, give him his dues, he changes tack smoothly. It's another hour before I leave the showroom, having paid a deposit, completed all the paperwork and arranged to pick the car up on Saturday afternoon after I've transferred the balance. I reckon that Dad would have struggled to get a better deal than I just have. I knew I wasn't going to get anything for the Micra, so I wasn't insulted by the £100 he offered for it in part-exchange, but I managed to get a decent discount on the Fiesta, along with the first two services thrown in, and the all-important floor mats.

'How did you get on? Did you buy anything?' my father asks when I get home.

'Yes, it was fine. I'm picking it up on Saturday.'

'Well, what is it?'

'Wait and see!' I can tell he's itching for me to say more and, in the end, I take pity on him. 'It's a Fiesta and it's blue, OK?'

'Good choice. Sensible, practical and the parts won't cost the earth. Did you get a discount? Did you remember to ask for the floor mats?'

I walk him through the freebies and he's impressed. 'Well done, Charley. You've got yourself a nice little runabout there, and you've obviously got your dad's knack for negotiation.'

I can't wait to see his face when I bring it home.

On Friday evening I set about clearing out the Micra. It's

amazing how much stuff accumulates in a car over time. The glovebox is full of leaflets from places that Josh and I have visited on our camping trips. I can't resist leafing through a few of them and letting the memories play in my mind. The cassettes are the same. I can remember Josh practically dancing with excitement when he found a copy of the very first *Now That's What I Call Music* album in a charity shop in Whitstable. 'This will be a collector's item one day, Charley!' he'd enthused. I won't miss it, or the Phil Collins albums, or the REO Speedwagon. The Whitney Houston tape that I'd wrenched out of the player on Christmas Day had worked its way under one of the seats, and takes a bit of dexterity to retrieve.

Eventually everything is out. I've kept a few useful things, like the antibacterial wipes and rubber gloves I found in the boot, but most of it is consigned to the bin. Reliving so much of Josh's and my shared history has been a bittersweet experience. It leaves me feeling a bit sad and hollow, but there are no tears this time. I think I'm coming to accept that maybe we had run our course. I still miss him, but he's right that we were arguing a lot and, if I'm honest with myself, I wasn't happy towards the end and he obviously wasn't – at least, not with me.

Saturday dawns. I'm in high spirits, looking forward to picking up the Fiesta as soon as I finish work. Typically, my first patient is late. I can see him sitting in his car in the car park, obviously talking on his phone. By the time he finally breezes in without so much as a word of apology, he's ten minutes late. He's followed by Mrs Howard and her two bratty kids. She always insists on a Saturday appointment, and always brings them. Why her husband can't look after them for a couple of hours I don't know. I have to try to keep one eye on what I'm doing and one eye on them, to make sure they aren't fiddling with my computer or any of my tools. After one very stressful appointment last year, I realised that I must have taken my eyes off them for just a fraction too long, as they'd added 'JULIAN IS A SMELLY BUM' and 'EMILY IS A BIGGER SMELLY BUM' to Mrs Howard's notes.

By the time I'm done, I'm running late for my appointment with Grant, and everyone on the road seems to be in dawdle mode, so when I finally pull up at the dealership I'm nearly half an hour late and my stomach is a knot of stress. Grant has an elderly couple at his desk as I walk into the showroom. He looks up, smiles and mouths 'I won't be long' at me, so I take a seat in the waiting area.

The elderly couple are taking an age. What on earth are they talking about? They seem to be going through the brochure on the desk word by word, and questioning everything. Eventually, they appear satisfied and Grant walks them out of the showroom.

'I'm so sorry,' he says as he collects me from the waiting area and leads me to his desk. 'They're a lovely couple, but they're struggling to make up their minds. That's the third time they've been in to look at the same car, would you believe?'

I apologise for my own lateness, but Grant tells me he'd been with the couple for an hour, so I would only have been waiting for longer. We start the handover process. There are a few more forms to fill in, and then he takes me out and shows me how everything on the car works. He helps me to connect my phone and shows me how I can control it from the screen in the car, and then I ease the Fiesta out onto the road for the journey home.

'Bloody hell, Charlotte, what is that?' My dad's jaw is on the floor as he comes out to inspect my purchase when I arrive home. 'When you said you'd bought a blue Fiesta, I thought you meant something sensible!'

'Don't you like it?'

He's walking round the car now, inspecting it. 'Of course I do. It's very smart and... good grief, look at the size of that spoiler! Have you turned into a boy racer?'

'It would be girl racer, and no. I just wanted something a bit more fun, you know?'

'Well, it's a long way from the Micra, I'll give you that. Is it as fast as it looks?'

I grin slyly at him. 'Oh yes.'

'Well, for God's sake don't tell your mother. She'll only worry about you.' He walks round the car one more time, then looks at me appraisingly for a moment, before breaking out a grin to match mine.

'I think it suits you perfectly.'

9

Mads and I are in Bluewater again, shopping for my 'holiday wardrobe' as she puts it. I was only after a swimsuit, but Mads has had other ideas. So far, she's talked me into three bikinis in different colours, with sarongs to go with them 'for when you're on your way to or from the beach'. I've also got a couple of suitcases, new sunglasses, a hat, some shorts and T-shirts, two pairs of sandals and a waterproof camera. On top of all of that, Mads persuaded me that I absolutely needed some light trousers and long-sleeved tops 'for the evenings', and I picked up some more clothes for my 'everyday' wardrobe. The floor around the table in the café where we're recuperating is covered in bags.

'So, I don't know if you want to hear this or not, but I bumped into Scarlett for the first time on the landing this morning,' Mads tells me, as she places a flat white and an almond croissant in front of me, and a slab of carrot cake and a pot of Earl Grey in front of herself.

I can feel my stomach knot. Do I want to know about Josh's

post-Charley love life? In the end curiosity gets the better of me.

'Oh yes?'

'Scrawny little bitch, isn't she?'

I laugh, and my stomach unclenches.

Mads takes a bite of her carrot cake and continues. 'She was letting herself into Josh's flat just as I was popping out for the papers and some milk. Short, scrawny, pointy-faced little thing. What on earth he sees in her I have no idea.'

Although I know she's doing it to be supportive, and I love her for it, her description isn't completely fair. I've met Scarlett a couple of times and, if I'm going to be as objective as I can be about the boyfriend-stealing bitch, a more accurate description of her would be 'petite'. She is a little bit pointy-faced but, in her favour, she has the most amazing mane of blonde wavy hair that reaches almost to her waist. I suspect a lot of colouring and styling goes into it, or else it's mostly extensions. An image of Josh running his hands through it as she straddles him pops into my head and I hastily push it away.

'Do you think she's moved in?' I ask.

'I don't know. She had a key, and she introduced herself to me as Josh's girlfriend, so she's obviously got her talons into him. Have you heard anything from him since Christmas?'

'Not a thing.'

'What a wanker.'

'Yup.'

'Listen, Charley, I don't know if it's too soon to start talking about this or not, but have you thought about how you're going to get back on the horse, so to speak?'

'In terms of boyfriends?'

'Yes.'

'I'm really not that fussed at the moment, Mads. I've got the holiday coming up, and then I'm moving into the flat. I think I just want a bit of time to be me before I get anyone else involved.'

'Fair enough. Let me know when you're ready to take the plunge, and we'll talk apps.'

Mads seems to have worked her way through most of the major dating apps over the years I've known her. She gets plenty of interest, but the lucky few who have made it beyond the first date have found themselves being given their marching orders before long. There was one guy, Mark, who looked promising, but even he only lasted for a couple of months before Mads declared that he was 'becoming a bit needy' and sent him on his way. She's also very territorial about her flat and has a firm rule that none of her boyfriends are allowed to stay the night, although she's quite happy to stay over with them. I asked her about it once, and she told me that letting someone stay over would lead to 'man stuff in the bathroom. Once that happens, they start seeing my flat as part of their territory and, before you know it, they're coming and going like they own the place, leaving their pants on the floor and you're doing their laundry. Ugh. My flat is my sanctuary, and it's staying that way.'

I'm not sure about the whole online dating thing. I've never done it, obviously, but I've heard plenty of tales from Mads and other friends about what it's like. From what I've heard, you spend ages creating a profile and trying to take a picture of yourself that doesn't make you look like you just escaped from Broadmoor, you put it online, and then you get contacted by loads of people you wouldn't go near in real life. 'Hi, darlin', my name's Ralph and I'm your dream date. Don't worry about the obvious mark where my wedding ring normally sits, let me send you a few dick pics to get you in the mood,' or 'Hi, I'm Dave. I've never had a girlfriend but I watch lots of porn and you look like you're up for it. How are you with large vegetables?' or even 'Hi, I'm Roger. My profile picture is of a good-looking bloke your age, but I'm actually seventy-two, bald and twenty-three stone.' Then there are the ones who appear to be reasonable prospects, and you spend hours messaging back and forth, only for them to disappear without a trace, leaving you wondering what you said wrong to make them 'ghost' you. Frankly, it sounds exhausting.

Mads interrupts my reverie. 'I know! What about a vibrator to keep you company while you're single? We could pop into Ann Summers after this. It'll be a fun way to finish our shopping trip.'

'Are you out of your mind?' I ask her incredulously. 'Apart from the fact that I think I'd be far too embarrassed to use it, I'm living with my parents for Christ's sake! Can you imagine if one of them walked past my bedroom and heard it buzzing or, God forbid, found it?'

'Charley, you're an adult woman and, last time I checked, you hadn't taken any vows of chastity. For all you know, your mum has one.'

'Do you have any idea how much I don't want that image in my head?'

Mads is undeterred. 'Also, there are some very quiet ones that your parents wouldn't hear even if they had their ears pressed against the door. You don't want your vagina to shrivel up from lack of use, do you?'

'You know that's not an actual thing, right?'

'Are you sure? You're willing to take that risk?'

'Yes. I really don't want a vibrator, thanks. Ask me again in six months, when I may be climbing the walls with sheer sexual frustration, but for now I'm fine.'

'OK. I guess you've always got your toothbrush in case of emergency.'

'Sorry, WHAT?'

'Oh, come on! Don't tell me you've never considered the sexual potential of an electric toothbrush. When I was at school nearly all the girls had them, and I'm certain it wasn't because they were hugely into dental hygiene.'

'Oh, Mads – eeuww!'

'Well, you've got to get your pleasures where you can when you're a hormonal adolescent. We weren't all lucky enough to go to co-educational schools like you, you know. At my school, your choices were limited to RSI, the toothbrush or rampant lesbianism. I'm sure boarding schools are some sort of mad social experiment dreamed up by a psychopath. Lock up six hundred sexually frustrated girls for five years and see what happens.'

She takes another bite of carrot cake. 'Didn't Josh ever suggest getting one, you know, to spice things up a bit?'

'God, no. Josh's idea of adventure was anything that deviated from the missionary position. I guess we found what worked for us and kept to that.'

'I see. Poor Scarlett.' She grins mischievously. 'Do you remember Adam?'

'Vaguely. Was he the tall, geeky one you went out with early last year?' An image of a fair-haired guy with glasses, wearing a white cable-knit jumper and black jeans comes to my mind. He must have lasted long enough for me to actually meet him.

'He bought me this rabbit vibrator – you know – the ones with the ears to stimulate your clitoris? He was desperate to try it. I tell you, Charley, the thing was massive – you could probably use it to spit-roast someone. Anyway, it was awful, like being attacked by a road-drill. It was definitely the death knell for him and me. The egg was fun though – I've still got that.'

'The egg? Do I want to know?'

'Oh yes.' She leans forward conspiratorially and lowers her voice, which I'm relieved about as I'm sure some of the people on the tables adjacent to ours have stopped talking and are listening to us.

'So, the egg is a little egg-shaped vibrator that you pop up inside you. It's got a remote control to start and stop it. You can put it in and get on with life as normal, then turn it on with the remote to give yourself a thrill. Steve bought it for me. He used to take me to the pub and set it off while we were having a drink. Someone actually asked me if I was OK on one occasion. I was biting my lip trying not to cry out, gripping the table and apparently I was bright red in the face. I think they were worried I was having a seizure.' She smiles at the memory.

* * *

A few days later, I'm eating my lunch in the staffroom at work when I notice an unread text on my phone. Clicking the icon, I see it's from Josh. I stare at it for a while without opening it. I can see the preview, which is 'Hi Charley, hope UR OK. Have...' Have what? Have you found out that Scarlett has given me chlamydia and you should get yourself checked? Have you seen the TV remote control? Have you realised that you're the bloody love of my life and I've chucked her out? I don't even know how I'd feel about that one any more. If he'd have sent it, I don't know, a week or two after we split, I probably would have rushed back. But now? I'm not so sure.

I tap to get the rest of the message, and read:

Hi Charley. Hope UR OK. Have packed up a few things that you left behind. Do you want to collect them or shall I give them to Madison to pass on to you? Josh x

Bastard! Nearly six weeks of total silence, and he breaks it with this? The text he should have sent would have said:

Hi Charley. I'm sorry that I'm such a fucking cliché. I'm sorry that I ruined what we had. I'm a weak, worthless human being. You deserve so much better than me. I've found a few items that you might like from the flat and, because I'm totally unworthy to be associated with anything to do with you, I wondered if you might like them? I can arrange for them to be delivered anywhere you'd like, at a time to suit you. Just tell me and I'll make it happen. You were the best thing that ever happened to me, and I can't believe I was stupid enough to be tempted by that useless tart Scarlett. I will spend the rest of my days mooning over a picture of the two of us, and playing songs that remind me of you. Josh (no kiss as I wouldn't dare)

I'm not upset. I'm livid. We were together for over ten years, which, when you think about it, is longer than many marriages last for. And this is all I get? 'Hey babe, you're done. Come and get your stuff.' I don't bloody think so.

I start several texts, varying in style from '*I can't believe you could send me something so callous after everything we shared*' (bit needy) to '*Fuck you!*' (bit over-aggressive and doesn't actually answer the question, even if it sums up how I'm feeling perfectly). I could ignore it, I suppose, but then Scarlett might feel justified in binning the 'stuff', whatever it is. This is enough to bring me back to earth, and I make a mental inventory of the things I left behind. From what I can remember there are a few CDs that I've probably already got on Spotify, some pictures of us that I definitely don't want, a couple of kitchen gadgets that will be easy to replace, and a sleeping cat stuffed toy that I bought as a surrogate pet a few years ago. Definitely nothing that I can't live without, and nothing worth crawling back to his flat as the dumped ex-girlfriend for. In the end my reply is short and to the point:

I have everything I need. Suggest you bin it.

I press 'send' and watch as it goes.

10

The taxi comes at 5.30 a.m. to get us to the airport on time for our early morning flight. I feel slightly disconnected from myself and muzzy as we leave, probably because it's been such a short night. It's dark, cold and raining as we leave home, and I feel slightly foolish as I shiver in just a T-shirt under my coat.

It seems that Mum and Dad have had another one of their upgrades since I last came on holiday with them. I had prepared for eight hours in economy class. I have my inflatable pillow round my neck and I've cast aside my skinny jeans in favour of some tracksuit bottoms that will be much more comfortable in the cramped space. However, when we get to the airport, Dad steers me away from the long check-in queue that I was joining without thinking, towards the business class check-in area, where there is nobody in front of us. We check in, whisk through fast-track security and head straight into the business class lounge.

I've never been in a business class lounge before and I feel distinctly underdressed. Everyone else here, apart from my parents, seems to be wearing either work suits or expensive designer outfits. The whole place has a sort of reverential hush about it, rather like you get in a library. Even the (very few) children are quiet. Conversations are conducted in murmurs, and the staff float around, silently collecting used cups and plates. A few people are helping themselves to the complimentary food and drink. I'm horrified to see a man mixing himself what looks like a pretty stiff gin and tonic. I want to go up to him and say, 'For goodness' sake, it's seven in the morning, what's wrong with you?'

Dad sees me staring and murmurs, 'I know it looks odd, Charlotte, but for all you know it might be midnight where he's come from. I'm going to grab some breakfast and a coffee. Coming?'

I follow him over to the area where the food and drink is situated. There is quite a selection to choose from – fruit, pastries, even hot food. 'I'm only going to have something small to keep me going,' Dad says. 'They'll feed us again on the plane.' I select a croissant and a flat white from the coffee machine and wander back to where we're sitting. It's all very nice and luxurious in here, but something is missing, and it takes me a while to put my finger on what it is.

Outside, in the main part of the airport, there's a buzz and a collective sense of anticipation. Everyone is going somewhere and, for the most part, they're excited and looking forward to it. I smiled as I saw what was obviously a wedding party; they were all wearing bright yellow T-shirts emblazoned with their role. I didn't see the bride herself, but I clocked the groom, the mother of the bride and the best man. They were loud in the way that happy, excited people are.

There's none of that in here. Everyone wears an air of studied indifference, as if they're saying, 'Yeah, this is nothing special. I do this all the time. I belong here.' I take a bite of my croissant and continue looking around. I definitely don't belong here.

'So, when did you guys start flying business class?' I ask my parents, after I've finished the croissant and washed it down with the coffee.

'It was a couple of years ago now,' Mum replies. 'Your dad was finding the economy class seats a little "restrictive", shall we say. I hoped it might get him thinking about losing weight, but of course his solution was to move to a bigger seat. We did premium economy one year, but then your dad decided we should go the whole hog and so now we fly business. It turns the flight into part of the holiday, rather than something you endure to get where you're going. It's also nice on the overnight flight back, because you can lie down and get some sleep. It's a lot of money, of course, but now that Simon, Emma and the girls don't come with us the overall cost of the holiday isn't much more.'

If I was unsure about the lounge, the flight part is more than enough to convince me that business class is where I want to be from now on. When the plane is ready to board, we walk down to the gate and we're let on first. There's no fighting over space in the overhead lockers as there are more than enough to go around, and then there's the seat itself. It's not so much a seat as a little pod in which you're cocooned. There's a blanket, pillow, amenity kit and a set of noise-cancelling head-phones on the seat when I arrive. I'm not quite sure what to do with these so I stuff them into the overhead locker for now.

When I sit down, I find that I can put my legs straight out in front of me and still not touch the seat in front. I've got a little storage drawer that I pop my shoes into. The TV screen is tucked into the wall of my pod but pops out at the press of a button. It's awesome.

A stewardess appears with a tray. 'Would you like champagne, orange juice or water, madam?' My earlier scruples disappear, and I happily accept a glass of champagne. Anyway, it's OK to drink champagne at breakfast, isn't it? There's a partition between me and the seat next to me, where my dad is sitting. I lower it and chink glasses with him.

'This is amazing, I could get used to this!' I enthuse.

'I know. I can't believe I spent all those years cramped up in the back of the plane. This is a much better way to travel.'

After take-off, the cabin crew come round with more drinks. I accept another glass of champagne – I'm on holiday after all – and have a look at the lunch menu. There are four choices of starter, three mains, and then a choice of a couple of puddings or cheese to finish. There's even a wine list. I decide I'll have pea and mint soup with chive crème fraiche to start, followed by seared fillet of cod with butter beans and chorizo for my main, and a warm caramel lava sponge with crème anglaise for pudding. I have no idea what the last one is, but I spotted the word caramel and decided I didn't need to know any more than that. The stewardess takes my order and then returns with a tablecloth that she carefully lays over my fold-out table. She proceeds to lay it out with cutlery and a napkin, and I feel like I'm in an upmarket restaurant rather than on a plane. The food is amazing. Each dish is served separately on bone china and looks like it's been prepared by a Michelin-starred chef. The lava cake turns out to be a sponge with a liquid caramel filling, and it's heavenly.

After lunch I retrieve the headphones, blanket and pillow from the overhead locker and settle back to watch a couple of films, and then afternoon tea is served shortly before we start our descent into Antigua. Normally by this point of a long flight I'm itching for it to be over so I can uncurl my body and start to feel human again, but here I'm savouring every moment of the experience. I can see what Mum means about it turning the flight into part of the holiday.

As I walk down the steps from the plane to the tarmac after we land, the warm Caribbean breeze caresses my body and I fight the urge to turn my face up to drink in the sun; falling arse over tit is not the way I want to start my holiday. The business class passengers are let off the plane first, so we pass pretty much straight through immigration to the baggage collection hall. Our bags are among the first off, and I smile when I notice that my suitcases each have a pink 'Priority' label on them. I could definitely get used to this.

The journey to our hotel takes about an hour, and I spend the whole time with my nose practically pressed against the window. The sea is that amazing shade of blue that I've only seen in travel brochures, and the white sandy beaches are pristine. On one of them a group of young men, stripped to the waist, are playing football. They're lean, dark-skinned and seem to radiate with life. Periodically, we pass shacks by the side of the road, selling either fruit, cold drinks, or hot food. People are milling around them, passing the time of day. The houses are painted bright colours, but a lot of them appear rather ramshackle to my British eyes and I can't help thinking they'd be very cold in winter, before I remember that this is the Caribbean and it's warm all year round. The vegetation is a rich, dark green, completely different to the golden brown that I remember from summer holidays in the South of France. Dad sees me looking at it and chuckles. 'There's a reason why it's so green. It's not called rainforest for nothing. You'll see.'

At last we arrive at the hotel. The reception area has a roof but no walls, so you can see straight through it to the gardens beyond. We're offered rum punch while Dad fills in the documentation, and then we are taken to our rooms, which are next door to each other. In comparison to the warmth outside my room is cool. The floor is a sort of marble, and feels cold and smooth under my bare feet. In the middle of the room is a modern, four-poster bed with two very fluffy-looking towels neatly arranged at the end. I discover a fridge, packed with bottles of ice-cold water. The bathroom is covered in marble tiles and has a bath, shower and two separate basins in front of the mirror.

By the time I've unpacked, it's late afternoon and the sun is beginning to set. I bang on my parents' door and we arrange to meet for drinks at the bar at seven, giving me an hour to kill. I decide to spend it exploring.

The hotel is located at the end of a peninsula and I quickly discover that, as well as a large pool with a swim-up bar, there are two beaches. One faces the Atlantic, and is quite breezy, and the other the much calmer Caribbean. I take off my sandals and curl my toes into the warm sand as I walk along the Caribbean beach. I can't resist a little paddle, and the water is clear and warm. There are lots of sunbeds, all empty by this time of day. I decide this is where I'll spend the bulk of my time. Mum and Dad have said I can do whatever excursions I like but, at the moment, the idea of just lying here with a good book and occasionally wandering into the sea for a swim seems perfect. The cicadas are warming up for their evening concert and I can feel my body relaxing as I head back to my room to get ready for dinner.

I meet Mum and Dad at the bar. They've both got cocktails, with bits of fruit in and those little umbrellas sticking out of the glass.

'What are you having, Charlotte?' Dad asks as I scan the array of bottles.

'I don't know. Maybe I'll just have a glass of white wine.'

'Well, that's fine if you want, but as you're in the Caribbean you might want to try something with rum in it. Why not start simple, with a rum and Coke?'

'You're right. OK, I'll have one of those. Thanks, Dad.'

He goes up to the bar to order it, and the barman brings it over to me. It tastes of Coke, but with an undercurrent of heat from the rum. It's delicious and I drink my way through two before we head off to the restaurant for dinner. The hotel has three restaurants: there's a self-serve buffet, which is where we're heading tonight, a restaurant down at the water's edge that specialises in seafood, and an Asian-style place that seems incongruous in this setting, but is very good, according to Mum and Dad.

'How many times have you been here?' I ask over dinner.

'This is our fifth time. We absolutely love it here, and when Emma and Simon came there was really good childcare and babysitting for the girls, so they were able to spend time together and relax. I love my granddaughters, but they can be pretty full on.' Mum smiles indulgently.

By the time we've finished eating, the jet lag has kicked in properly and I'm struggling to keep my eyes open. I head back to my room, crawl into the sumptuous bed and fall into a blissful sleep.

11

The jet lag wakes me very early the next morning. I've arranged to meet Mum and Dad for breakfast at eight, but I have two hours to kill before then, so I turn over and close my eyes to see if I can go back to sleep. From the sounds of it Mum and Dad are awake too. I can hear their voices through the wall. It doesn't sound like conversation though, there's too much of a rhythm to it. There's something not right about it, but I'm not quite able to put my finger on what it is. Suddenly it dawns on me, and I sit bolt upright in bed.

OhGodOhGodOhGod... I'm listening to my parents having sex.

Hastily, I reach for the remote control and switch on the TV. It automatically goes to a channel showing some terrible American comedy with canned laughter, but I don't care. Anything to drown out the noises from the next room. How on earth am I going to be able to face them at breakfast after this? An imaginary conversation plays out in my head:

'Morning, Mum, morning, Dad. That was some noisy sex you two were having. Was it good?'

'Very nice, thanks, Charlotte. Would you like tea or coffee?'

Maybe I could sneak out and have breakfast early, in order to avoid them? That might hurt their feelings though, particularly as it's our first morning here. I have another horrific thought: is this going to be my dawn chorus for the whole two weeks we're here? I think that would be enough to give any child PTSD. I wonder if they sell earplugs in the shop? I make a mental note to check it out later.

I decide to get up and have a long shower. I'm wide awake now so there's no point in trying to go back to sleep. Also, the noise of the shower will further insulate me from my amorous parents. I grab a towel and pad into the bathroom, shutting the door behind me for extra sound insulation. Obviously, I'm happy *in concept* that my parents are still enjoying an active love life, in the same way that I'm happy *in concept* that some people find oysters delicious. In practice I find both oysters and the stark reality of my parents having sex rather nauseating.

As I stand under the shower, I try to focus on the day ahead and make some sort of a plan. It doesn't take long, consisting mainly of lying around either dozing or reading a book, swimming in the sea and generally watching the world go by, punctuated by meals. I might wander up to reception at some point and see what excursions are on offer. Oh, and earplugs – mustn't forget those.

After I've showered, washed and conditioned my hair and dried it using the rather under-powered hotel dryer, I slather myself in factor fifty sun cream and put on one of my new bikinis, with a pair of shorts and a T-shirt over the top. Tentatively, I turn down the volume of the TV and I'm reassured to hear what sounds like normal conversation from next door. There's still well over an hour before we're due to go for breakfast, so I grab my book and head out onto my balcony to read. It obviously rained overnight, and the grass is sparkling in the morning sunshine. Although it's still very early, the air is warm and humid, and filled with the sounds of unfamiliar insects and birds. Hotel staff are pulling large trolleys of laundry into position, getting ready for the day's cleaning. I spot a couple of guests out for an early morning run. It's a world away from the freezing February we left behind, and it feels slightly unreal.

After I've watched the view for a while, I pad back into my room to make a cup of coffee. It's instant, and not very nice, but it will tide me over until I hopefully get a decent cup at breakfast. As I take it outside, I hear the door of my parents' room open and someone steps out onto the adjacent balcony. There's a barrier between us, so I can't see who it is, but I'm not left wondering for long.

'Morning, Charlotte,' Dad's voice says.

'Morning!' I reply. In trying to keep my voice as normal and upbeat as possible, I realise I'm speaking about an octave higher than usual.

'Did you sleep OK?' he asks.

Normal voice, Charley, come on. You can do this. It's a lot easier when you're not looking at him. 'Yes, the bed is super-comfy. I woke up pretty early because of the jet lag, but I expect that will settle down.'

'Yes, give it a couple of days and you'll be fine. Well, bang on our door at eight and we'll go and find some breakfast, shall we?'

I pick up my book and make a start. It's a kind of whodunnit with a bit of romance thrown in. Perfect holiday reading.

At eight o'clock, I knock on Mum and Dad's door and we set off to the buffet restaurant where breakfast is laid out. There are cereals, pastries, a selection of fruit, a hot buffet and a choice of hot and cold drinks. I help myself to some fruit and yoghurt; the hot buffet looks very tempting but if I'm not going to be doing any exercise I'll put on loads of weight if I'm not careful. Plus, I'm not sure I'm that hungry after the events of the morning so far. Mum is very bright-eyed and bushy-tailed, chatting away about this and that as she puts things on her plate. I try to follow her conversation, but can't quite bring myself to look her in the eye yet.

'Are you OK, Charlotte? You're very quiet this morning!' she remarks after we've finished helping ourselves and returned to our table.

No, of course I'm not OK! I heard you two 'at it' and I'm mortify-ingly embarrassed! 'Yes, I'm fine thanks. Just, you know, taking it all in.'

I force myself to look at her. Immediately an image of her stark-naked and bouncing around on top of Dad comes into my mind and I struggle to push it out again.

'Well, as long as that's all it is. Have you thought about what you might like to do today?'

'I thought I might go and find a spot on the Caribbean side, start working on my tan. What about you two?'

'We're going to go to the spa and see if we can get ourselves booked in for a massage. They do fabulous massages here. We thought we'd have one of those couple's ones, where you both get massaged at the same time.'

We finish our breakfast and, by the end, I'm back on a reasonably even keel. We agree to meet back at the bar in the evening and head back to our rooms to get ready for the day. I change out of the shorts and T-shirt and wrap one of the sarongs around me, before grabbing my book, sun cream, sunglasses (vital for surreptitious people-watching) and hat, and head off to the beach.

There are many more people here than yesterday evening, but still plenty of sunbeds available. I spot a free pair under an umbrella and make a beeline for them. They're in the first row, nearest the sea so it will only be a few steps to the water when I want to cool down. Plus, if I get a bit hot, I can move myself under the shade of the umbrella. I spread my towel out on the right-hand bed and pop all my other bits and pieces on the other one, within easy reach. Then I lie back and pick up my book once again.

I polish off a few more chapters, with occasional breaks to watch my fellow guests. Some have obviously been here a while; they have deep tans and lie in full sunlight, toasting themselves. Others, like me, are still pale and being careful with the sun. I spot one woman fighting a losing battle with her children. She evidently wants them to keep their shirts on, but they keep taking them off and running away from her, laughing. People are heading out onto the water in kayaks, pedaloes and on windsurf boards. There's a nice breeze, enough to power the windsurfers along at a reasonable pace. One man is having a water-skiing lesson. I'm guessing he hasn't done it before as, every time he comes up out of the water, he falls flat on his face back into it. The instructor is encouraging him from the rear of the boat, and a woman I guess is either his wife or girlfriend is also in the boat, taking pictures.

As I'm watching them, I become aware of a shadow falling over me. I look up to see a man standing there, looking at me slightly quizzically.

'Mrs Wells, I presume?' he asks.

'Umm, sorry?'

'Sorry, bad joke,' he says, registering my confusion. 'You probably didn't notice, but these two sunbeds are reserved for the honeymoon suite. I'm Ed, by the way – Ed Wells.'

'Oh shit, I'm so sorry!' I say, hastily gathering my stuff together. 'I didn't realise. I didn't see any sign. Please apologise to your wife for me.' My embarrassment is making me gabble.

He plonks himself down on the other sunbed. 'Relax,' he says. 'There's no rush. Please stay as long as you like. I can promise you my wife won't need the sunbed. To be honest, I'd be glad of the company.' He makes quotation marks with his fingers when he says the word 'wife'.

Oh no. They've obviously had a massive row and he's come down here to cool off. If that's happening on the honeymoon it doesn't bode well for the rest of the marriage.

I've read about couples who split up not long after their honeymoons, and I kind of see how that might happen. You get engaged, you start planning this massive wedding and it kind of takes over to the point where everything is about the wedding. Then it happens, and it's amazing, and you jet off to somewhere exotic for your honeymoon, and that's all perfect too, and then you come back to your mundane semi-detached in Croydon, or wherever, and suddenly it's all very grey and ordinary. Soon, everything about the person who you thought was perfect only a few months ago annoys you. They're leaving the toilet seat up, or failing to notice that the bin needs emptying. You start sniping at each other, and before long you're wondering what on earth you saw in each other.

I can understand that, but to be at each other's throats on honeymoon, when you're supposed to still be in the loved-up haze of the whole wedding experience? That's a big, flashing, bright red warning light if you ask me.

He doesn't look or sound like he's just had a blazing row with someone though. In fact, I'd call his tone more 'resigned'. Of course, there could be a different explanation. Maybe she's gone off to the spa and he's feeling neglected and a bit pissed off, so he's decided to use my company to pass the time. It doesn't exactly give the right impression though, talking to other women the moment his new wife's back is turned.

I take a moment to study him. He has fair hair, a few laughter lines around his brown eyes, and a wide mouth that reveals even, white teeth when he smiles. His body is, well, male. He's no bodybuilder, but he's obviously in pretty good shape. I would estimate him to be in his mid-thirties. Mrs Wells, whoever she is, has bagged herself a pretty good specimen physically, at least.

'I don't think that's a good idea,' I tell him. 'I don't know where your wife is or how long she's planning to be, but I don't imagine she'd be very pleased to find you chatting to some strange woman that you've given her sunbed to, even if she's not planning to use it herself, do you?'

'I don't think she'd mind, actually.'

What kind of wife wouldn't mind her husband spending time with another woman on her honeymoon? Unless – a thought pops into my head – maybe they're one of those couples who have an 'open' relationship, and he's free to do what he wants as long as he tells her about it afterwards. Well, if that's the case, I'm definitely not hanging around. That kind of thing is completely not my scene.

It takes me a moment to realise he's still speaking.

'You see, she's not here. In fact, I have no idea where she is.'

12

'What do you mean, you have no idea where she is? She must be in the hotel somewhere.'

'As far as I know she's still in the UK. Let me start from the beginning, then things might make a bit more sense. Is that OK with you?'

How can I resist? This sounds like it'll be an interesting story at least, and it's not like I've got anywhere else I need to be. 'Sure,' I say, and settle back onto the sunbed.

'Have you heard of the TV programme *Married Before We Met*?'

I know it well. Mads and I have watched every series avidly. Josh watched one episode and refused to watch any more, so I used to go over to Mads' apartment with a bottle of wine each week when it was on. She would either cook or one of us would get a takeaway, and we would sit and watch it together.

'I have watched it, yes,' I tell him.

'I applied for it and was matched up with someone.'

'Oh, wow! What made you enter?'

'Well, I'm thirty-four and, apart from one brief relationship, I've been single since I left university. My job is pretty
demanding, and I guess the nature of what I do is a bit off-
putting if you're swiping through Tinder, or whatever the
nation's favourite dating app is these days. So I thought I'd put
myself in, submit myself to the science, as they like us to say,
and see what happened.'

'What's your job?' I try to envision him in various unap-
pealing jobs – in an abattoir, covered in blood, or in a sewage
pipe, covered in shit. Neither seem to work very well, and I
notice his hands look soft, so probably not a job that involves
lots of manual labour.

'I'm a divorce lawyer.'

I burst out laughing. 'I can see why that might kill the
romantic vibe! So, what happened? I'm trying to envision you
doing one of those pieces to camera about why you'd been
single for a long time but wanted to meet "the one" so decided
to see if science could help you.'

He smiles. 'I can see you *really* know the show.'

'Oh yes. Don't you?'

'No. Well, I didn't before I applied.'

'Ah. Do you not think a bit of research might have been a
good idea? It's pretty full on.'

'They sent me an information pack with the application
form. I thought that explained everything pretty well.'

'What did it say?'

'That I'd have a load of interviews with various relationship experts, and I'd have to fill in questionnaires about my
personality, the kind of person I was looking for, and so on. I
had to agree to all of it being filmed, even if I wasn't chosen for

the show. Once I'd attended my selection panel, as they called it, they would be in touch if they thought they'd found a match.'

'Yes, they show you that bit right at the beginning. I always think it looks like one of those talent shows, with long queues of people hoping to become the next big thing.'

'There were masses of people there, and mine was just one of several selection panels that they conducted around the country. Apparently, over five thousand people apply every year.'

'Wow. I never knew it was as popular as that.'

'Me neither, until I turned up. It was really intense. As well as the interviews and the endless questionnaires, they also measured me. Not just height and weight, but pretty much every part of me. Apparently, there's some scientific theory that reckons you match well with people who have similar relative body dimensions.'

'And the woo-woo science didn't ring any alarm bells?'

'It did sound a bit made up, I'll grant you. They were thorough though; the selection panel took the whole day.'

'Did they give you any indication of what would happen if you were selected?'

'That was all in the pack. It said that successful applicants would be told the first name of the person they were marrying, and given a location and time for the wedding. It explained the format of the ceremony, that there would be a screen between us until after we'd said our vows, so we couldn't see each other until we were married. We'd be given a budget for wedding clothes, and they would take care of the wedding venue and all the costs associated with the reception and so on.'

'Hm. It seems like they glossed over some significant details, but carry on.'

'After the reception, they would put us up in a hotel for the night, and then send us somewhere nice on honeymoon to get to know each other better. After the honeymoon, we would move in together for six weeks in a flat they would provide, and there would be various tasks assigned to help us fast-track the relationship. We would check in with the experts every week so they could help with any problems, and all being well we'd want to stay together at the end. It sounded really interesting.'

'And that's all they told you?'

'Pretty much.'

'OK, they left out some pretty important things. For example, how many of these relationships stay the course, do you think?'

'I don't know. They didn't say.'

'I'm sure they didn't! I've watched four series so far and, to my knowledge, there is only one couple that's still together. It's pretty much car-crash TV, and the only reason I watch it is because I'm hoping against hope that some of the couples will make it. Some of them don't even get to the end of the honeymoon; there was a woman in the last series who hated her husband so much, she waited until he'd gone out, left him a goodbye note and paid for her own flight home! And then there are the families and friends, who seem determined to derail even the best functioning marriages. I remember one guy's mother tearing into a poor bride because she didn't do all the cooking and laundry for her precious boy. Did you really think you would find true love in a show like that?'

'Well, like I said, I didn't really do any research,' he admits, sheepishly. 'I literally only saw a trailer where they were asking people to apply, and I thought, why not? It seemed as good a way of finding someone as any.'

'I bet they loved you. A lamb to the slaughter, if you don't mind me saying.'

'I'll take your word for it. To be honest, having seen how many people were applying, I reckoned I had zero chance of getting on, so I pretty much forgot all about it. Four weeks later, they rang me up and told me they'd matched me with someone called Sarah.'

'How did you feel when they rang?'

'I was over the moon, but also scared. Suddenly it all became real, if you know what I mean. They gave me the option of not going ahead but, once I'd had a bit of time to think about it, I decided that I should go through with it. I think if I'd have said no, I'd always have been wondering whether I'd missed out on the perfect person for me.'

'I'm going to let you off that remark as you'd never seen the show. So, you accepted.'

'I did, and then we had to go for a much more detailed presentation, where we had talks on safeguarding, mental health, consent, grievance procedures and that kind of thing. Basically, the production company was covering itself in case any of us turned out to be psychopaths or rapists. That's how I read it.'

'Still no alarm bells?'

'No. Working in the legal profession, I would have been quite surprised if they hadn't done it. It wasn't all doom and gloom.' He smiles. 'There were also some fascinating presentations on the allowable expenses, how to claim them and so on, as well as explanations on when the film crew needed to be with us.'

'It sounds riveting.' I laugh. 'Were you all together then? What was it like looking at the women and wondering which one was your wife?'

'No, they did the sessions for the men and women separately.'

'I guess that makes sense. It would be awful if you really took against one of the women at the presentation and then found out you'd married her! Actually, maybe it wouldn't be any worse than the reaction of some of the people in the previous series when they first clapped eyes on their new partner. What happened next?'

'The first thing they wanted to film was me telling my friends and family that I was going to marry someone I'd never met. Do you have any idea how much grilling you get when you ring people and invite them over to share some important news in front of a film crew?'

'I've never thought about it.'

'My mum was the worst. She kept saying, "Just tell me what's going on, Ed. Are you in any trouble?" and, of course, I couldn't even give her a clue.'

'How did they react when you told them?'

'I think it's best described as...' he pauses '...mixed.'

'Go on.'

'The first thing is that everyone knows something must be up, because of the whole camera crew thing, so they're all on edge. I think my parents were hoping I'd landed some massive job that was going to make the news, so they'd geared themselves up for that and were very disappointed when I told them what I was really doing. Luckily, my sister thought it was brilliant and helped me to talk them round. My friends and colleagues at work mostly thought it was pretty cool when I told them. Luckily, I didn't have the camera crew with me when I told my boss, as he wasn't wild about it at all; he thought it might bring the firm into disrepute, so I had to promise never to mention where I worked on the show. My PA, Alice, was also horrified.'

'What's it got to do with her?'

'Nothing, I suppose. It just surprised me, because she's normally one of those incredibly efficient people who just get on with the work and don't express opinions.'

'What did she say?'

'She basically told me I needed someone who understood the particular pressures of what I do, was prepared to play second fiddle to my work, wouldn't make unreasonable demands on me, and that I was crazy if I thought I would find someone like that in a reality TV show.'

'Hm. We call women like that "doormats". How did your boss feel about the fact that you wanted, what, eight weeks off?'

'Why would I want that?' He looks confused.

'When you're living in the flat, if you make it that far, you don't work, do you?'

'Yes. They only film you in the evenings and at weekends. The rest of the time is yours. I arranged some remote working as I didn't know where the flat would be, but I made it clear when I signed up that I would need to be in the office at least two days per week.'

'Oh. The way they show it makes you think that you're together all the time.'

'That would be incredibly intense and not very realistic, don't you think? Also, I can't think of many people who can just drop their jobs for eight weeks. It would seriously limit the pool of applicants.'

'I suppose so. So, you've had the interviews, they've matched you with Sarah, and you've had awkward conversations with your friends and family in front of the camera. What happened next?'

'The production company take care of all the practicalities, so all I needed to do was get all my wedding clobber, morning coat and so on, and appoint a best man. I also bought some diamond earrings as a "hello" gift for Sarah. Probably a bit of a cliché, but you have no idea how difficult it is to buy a romantic present for someone you've never met. I wrote a speech for the wedding about how delighted I was, even though I had no idea if I would be delighted or not. It was all a bit surreal, I can tell you. By the time the wedding day came around I was in knots. Part of me was really excited that I could be about to meet the woman I was going to spend the rest of my life with, and part of me was kicking myself for being stupid enough to sign up for something like this.'

'Talk me through the wedding day.'

'OK. Our wedding was in a hotel near Gatwick Airport, and they put my best man and me up there the night before. We spent the morning getting dressed up in our wedding gear, I had to do various pieces to the camera about how I was feeling about the wedding and so on, and then we went down into the function room where the ceremony was going to be held. It's just like you see on the TV, with the screen and every-thing. I was all in my finery, my friends and family were all there, and we could hear Sarah's family through the screen but, of course, we couldn't see them. The celebrant was there, and all the camera crew and their equipment. Because of the screen, there were two crews: one to film on her side, and one to film on mine. The wedding was scheduled for two o'clock, but it's a bride's prerogative to be late, isn't it, so when two fifteen came and went I didn't think anything was particularly unusual. By two thirty the guests were getting restless, and so was I.'

'Yes, that's getting towards rudely late. What time did she finally arrive?'

'She never turned up at all.'

13

'What? That's awful, Ed. I'm so sorry.'

'Yup. The crew saw the car pull up and then drive away again, so they rang the chauffeur to find out what was going on. Apparently, her dad had been violently against it from the moment she told him what she was planning. She didn't let that put her off to start with, but he did such a number on her while they were in the car on the way to the venue that, by the time she got there, she'd decided she didn't want to go through with it after all.'

'You must have been gutted.'

'I felt pretty foolish. You hear stories of people being stood up at the altar, but I never imagined that it would happen to me. Thankfully, the people from the production company were really good. They took me off into a side room to explain what had happened, and also dealt with the guests for me, so I didn't have to face anyone. I wasn't heartbroken – how could I be when I'd never even met her? But I was really disappointed, after everything I'd been through and all the build-up.'

'What happened about the reception and stuff though? That must all have been booked and paid for?'

'Do you know, I have no idea. Maybe the guests went anyway. As soon as it was clear the wedding wasn't going ahead, the guy from the production company told me I had a choice. I could either leave the show there and then, which they'd quite understand, or, because I'd entered in good faith, they were happy for me to go to the hotel we were supposed to be spending our wedding night in, and then come on the honeymoon by myself. They would send a crew to check in with me at various points, for the show, but other than that I'd be able to enjoy the holiday uninterrupted. It was a no-brainer. Face down the pity and "I told you so's", or run away and let the dust settle a bit. I'd already booked the time off work, so here I am. Anyway, enough about me. I realise I've spent the last however long boring you with my story, and I don't even know your name!'

'Not boring at all! I'm Charlotte, but only my parents call me that. Most people call me either Charley, Lottie or Lots. Frankly, I also respond pretty well to "Oi!", so you can take your pick.'

'I like Charlotte, but I don't want to sound like your dad, so I think I'll go with Charley, if it's all the same to you. So, Charley, what's your story? The way you had your stuff spread out indicates to me that you weren't expecting anyone to join you.'

'You can't possibly infer that!' I exclaim, laughing. 'I might be using my stuff to save the sunbed for my hot, ripped boyfriend. For all you know he's on his way now, and when he sees you talking to me, he's going to beat the crap out of you.'

Ed raises his eyebrows. He doesn't seem to have bought my story at all.

'OK, fair cop,' I say, 'I'm here on my own as well. Well, that's not strictly true. I'm here with my parents.'

Ed looks horrified. 'Oh God. I'm so sorry. I thought you were older...'

I laugh again. 'Relax! I'm twenty-seven. I broke up with my long-term boyfriend at Christmas, so Mum and Dad invited me to come to Antigua with them as part of my recovery. Who's going to turn down a bit of free sun and sand, especially when the weather at home is so horrible?'

'Fair point. May I ask what happened with the boyfriend, if that's not too personal? I've told you my story, so I'm ready to listen if you want to share yours.'

I tell him about Josh and me. I talk about how we met, how we started to argue after he got the job at Earthkind, and how we broke up. He's an attentive listener, and he asks lots of questions. I suspect it's the lawyer in him, but I find him very easy to talk to.

'So, tell me. Why a divorce lawyer?' I ask after I've filled him in on the collapse of my love life.

'Good question. On the face of it, it doesn't sound very appealing, does it? Lots of people base their understanding of lawyers on TV shows like *Suits*, where divorcing couples have full-on screaming matches in boardrooms while their respective lawyers try to referee. The reality is that scenes like that are pretty rare. Most of what I do is investigative stuff. My clients are all what we call "high net worth", and their primary goal is either to get their hands on as large a share of the pie as possible, or to hold on to as much of it as possible by hiding it from their spouse. Some of them go to extraordinary lengths to conceal their assets, so a lot of my job is tracking those down so that the whole estate can be divided up fairly.'

'Have you got any clients that I might know?'

'Do you remember the Didier Oponome divorce? It was widely reported in the papers.'

'Oh, yes. He's the Premier League footballer who couldn't keep it in his trousers. Eventually his wife, Madeleine, had enough and divorced him. From what I remember, she got millions.'

'Fifty-two million and enough loose change to buy a couple of Bentleys. Yes, I represented her.'

'Wow! What was she like?'

'I can't tell you about her specifically – client confidentiality and all that. What I can say is that, when people have that much money, it affects the way they view the world. They are used to getting whatever they want, whenever they want it, and they generally don't react very well if you tell them they can't have something.'

'I'll bet. Have you ever had to send someone away?'

'We try very hard not to do that. It's bad PR for the company. If someone is exceptionally demanding or difficult, I sometimes ask a colleague to join the case, to share the workload. Of course, the customer has to pay for that, but the extra amount is chicken feed in the overall scheme of things.'

'I bet it's lucrative though.'

'Well—' he smiles shyly at me '—let me put it this way. Without wanting to sound arrogant, I'm very good at what I do, and I therefore come at a high price.'

'Doesn't it put you off relationships though? When all of

your work is to do with break-ups, it must make you a little jaded and cynical, surely?'

'You'd think that, wouldn't you? But no, I've got lots of positive role models for marriage in my life – my parents, for example. I know the divorce statistics look depressing, but there are lots of marriages that work too. Where love is concerned, I'm definitely optimistic that the right person is out there for me, even if it's not Sarah.

'I think the biggest problem for me has been the long hours that I work. It's not unusual for me to be in the office until ten at night, or even later if we've got a particularly big case on. That doesn't leave a lot of time for meeting new people. At the weekends I often go to visit my parents, or I see friends, or I'm in my flat reviewing documents for the next week. The good news is that I'm now at a level where I can start to delegate more and hopefully get some work–life balance back. It's something I've been thinking about for a while, and I suppose I thought getting married would kick-start me into actually doing something about it. There's no great reason to leave the office if all you're going back to is an empty flat, but if you're sharing it with someone special...'

'Yeah, I get that. I'm moving into a flat after this holiday and, although it's lovely and I'm looking forward to having my own space again, it's going to be odd being on my own, particularly after living with Josh for so long.'

Ed busies himself arranging the towel on his sunbed and applying sun cream, so I pick my book back up and carry on reading. A companionable silence settles between us, punctuated with occasional bursts of conversation. When lunchtime comes, it seems only natural for us to wander up to the buffet together. I spot my parents already sitting down and I carefully steer Ed to a table away from theirs. I know we've shared a lot this morning, but I don't think I know him well enough to inflict my parents on him.

Of course, I should have known that would never work. I see my mother spot us sitting together, and her eyes are out on stalks. She nudges my dad and she's obviously telling him, 'Don't look now!' because he slowly turns round, trying to look as nonchalant as possible. He's a terrible actor, my dad.

'Just to warn you, my parents are sitting over there and they've clocked us,' I say to Ed. 'Ten to one they make a beeline for us as soon as they've finished eating.'

'Anything I need to know in advance?'

'My mum is very inquisitive, but otherwise I think they're pretty normal. You tell me afterwards.'

Sure enough, as soon as they've finished their meal, they make their way over.

'Charlotte!' exclaims my mother, mock disapprovingly. 'Why didn't you come and sit with us, and introduce us to your friend?'

I just about manage to resist rolling my eyes at Ed. 'Mum, this is Ed. We met on the beach this morning when I stole one of his sunloungers and we just got chatting. Ed, this is my mother, Christine, and my father, John.'

Ed is pure charm. He's straight on his feet shaking my parents by the hand, asking them if they're enjoying their holiday and generally buttering them up. My mother is practically cooing at him.

'We've booked a table at the seafood restaurant for this evening, Charlotte,' Dad says to me after a bit. 'You're more than welcome to join us, Ed, if my daughter has no objections and you'd like to. What do you say? Shall I tell reception we'll be a table of four rather than three?'

Talk about being put on the spot! I look at Ed, but I can't read his expression. 'That really is very kind of you,' he says after a short pause. 'I'd love to join you, as long as Charley doesn't mind.'

Poor Ed. He has no idea what he's letting himself in for. 'Fine with me!' I say, plastering a smile on my face.

'That's sorted then. I'll speak to reception. We'll meet in the bar for drinks at seven. See you both there.'

As they walk away, I can see them talking. My mother is particularly animated and I know she's pretty much married me to Ed already. I need to head this off to prevent an embarrassing situation.

'I'm so sorry about that,' I say to Ed. 'Please don't feel pressured by my parents. I'm happy to make an excuse on your behalf.'

He smiles. 'I'd love to hear that. What would you use? A prior engagement? I don't think that would come across as very believable, given that I'm on holiday, do you? I don't think anything short of drowning me would wash with your mother.'

'I'm sure I could arrange a drowning,' I say, mock-threateningly.

'Look, the last thing I want to do is put you in a difficult position. If me being there makes it awkward for you, I'm quite happy to develop a sudden illness. Perhaps I'll react badly to this delicious goat curry,' he offers.

I laugh. '"Ed discovered he's horribly allergic to goat,

shortly after devouring a whole plateful." That sounds even less plausible. I'm sorry but I'm going to have to drown you. It's for the best. You'll thank me later.'

As we walk back to the beach, I consider my predicament. I really don't want my parents to get the wrong idea and start trying to set us up, but, on the other hand, I'm really enjoying Ed's company. A question comes to my mind.

'Tell me something. If you weren't having dinner with us tonight, what would you be doing?'

'I've mostly been ordering room service so far. It's extra cost, but I have an expenses budget as part of the package. I've got a great view from my balcony, so I tend to sit out there and eat.'

'That sounds a bit shit if I'm honest, view or no view. If you'd really like to, I'd love you to join us tonight.'

14

The next morning, I spot Ed already on his sunbed as I walk across the beach. He looks up as I approach and smiles.

'Mrs Wells, I presume?'

'Ha ha. May I?' I indicate the sunbed next to his.

'Of course!'

The previous evening went much better than I'd feared. I warned Mum and Dad against trying to set us up, and they (mostly) behaved. Ed was there waiting for us when we arrived at the bar. He was dressed in a plain blue shirt with the sleeves rolled up, chinos, and boat shoes. As I sat down next to him, I got a whiff of his aftershave, which was woody and a bit spicy. He looked and smelled, well, *expensive*.

Mum and Dad had never heard of *Married Before We Met*, but were fascinated by it. 'Maybe we should enter you, Charlotte!' Dad had exclaimed at one point. I could see Mum watching us closely, looking for any hints that there might be a spark between Ed and me but, to her credit, she managed not to say anything inappropriate. Ed was attentive to both of them, asking my father about his business and being generally charming to Mum. The food was delicious, and we all drank slightly more than we ought to have done. At the end of the evening, as we tipsily made our way back to our rooms, Ed held me back at the point where his route parted from ours.

'I had a really lovely day today, Charley. Thank you so much.'

I smiled at him. 'I did too. See you tomorrow.' Without thinking I wrapped my arms around him in a quick hug and leaned up to kiss him on the cheek. As I continued back to my room, I caught the faintest whiff of his aftershave on me that I must have picked up when I hugged him.

It was only when I'd got back, brushed my teeth and had a long drink of water to stave off any potential hangover that I realised I'd completely forgotten to buy any earplugs. Thankfully there had been no dawn chorus from my parents this morning.

'I had a thought when I woke up, and I've got a proposal for you if you're up to it?' Ed says to me, after I've laid out my towel and got myself settled.

I try, and fail, to look stern. 'Look, mate. You might be into all this marrying people you've never met malarkey, but I'm an old-fashioned sort of girl. I only met you yesterday and you're wanting to propose already? Shouldn't you be wining and dining me a lot more first?'

'Not that sort of proposal!' He laughs. 'Here's the thing. As part of the whole honeymoon experience, Sarah and I were supposed to choose some activities from a list that the production company provided. I haven't done any of them as there didn't seem to be much point on my own, but I wondered whether you might like to have a go at some of them with me?'

I consider it for a moment. 'Have you got the list?'

He hands it over and I scan it:

- Water sports including water-skiing, kayaking and windsurfing
- A private 4x4 tour of the island with guide
- A boat trip including snorkelling and kayaking through the mangrove swamps
- A couple's massage at the hotel spa
- Parasailing
- A romantic picnic with a breathtaking view (strongly recommended)

'The water sports sound fun,' I say to Ed, 'and the tour of the island might be interesting.'

'Yes, I liked the sound of them,' he agrees.

'I'm not convinced by the boat trip though. Sounds like it's probably a booze cruise. The couple's massage is definitely out. Mum and Dad had one of those yesterday and told me that you pretty much have to strip off in front of each other before you lie down under the towels. Way too intimate.'

'Ah, damn,' says Ed with a wink, 'you've seen through my plan.'

'Behave! I'm not sure whether I'd enjoy parasailing, but how can I resist the romantic picnic with a breathtaking view?'

'I will have to let you down on that one, I'm afraid,' Ed replies. 'The fact is that the picnic is the only activity on that list that is organised by the production company directly and not through the hotel. As I'm not officially on honeymoon, they haven't arranged anything, so that one is not available. Leave it with me and I'll see if I can come up with something else though.'

I knew it. Of course the grooms don't organise it!

'Fair enough. Where do you want to start?'

By lunchtime we're organised. Incredibly, we've managed to get a water-skiing lesson booked for this afternoon as there was a cancellation. Tomorrow we're windsurfing in the morning and kayaking in the afternoon, then we have a day off before we go on the 4x4 tour of the island on Ed's last day before he flies home.

'Bugger, I think I've left something at reception,' Ed remarks as we get back to the beach. 'I'll just go and get it. Back in a mo.'

He's gone for a very long time and seems rather pleased with himself on his return.

'Did you find it?' I ask.

'Find what?' he replies.

'The thing you left at reception. Did you find it?'

'Oh, that! Yes, thanks. All good.'

There's definitely something fishy going on here. Not only was he gone far too long to just be collecting something he'd left behind, but he didn't come back carrying anything either.

'You were gone a long time,' I remark, casually.

'Sorry about that. There were a load of people checking in, and I had to wait.'

I'm sure he's lying. I just don't know why. Whatever it is, I'm not going to get it out of him by further questioning, so I decide to let it go for now.

By the end of the water-skiing lesson I've completely forgotten about it. There's so much to take in. The instructor explains how we have to position our bodies in the water, how to rise up as the boat starts to pull us, and how to get into a standing position. It all sounds very complicated, but the instructor assures me that it's easier than it sounds.

Ed suggests that I might like to go first. He claims that he's being gentlemanly, but I suspect he just wants to watch and try to pick up a few tips from my failures. Fine, I'll show him. I put on my life jacket, take the skis and march defiantly into the water.

Fifteen minutes later I feel like I've swallowed half of the bay. This is really hard! The bit the instructor didn't tell me on land is that, as soon as the boat has put tension on the rope, they hit full power to get you up and out of the water. The first time it happened, I was so surprised I let go of the rope and didn't go anywhere at all. The second and third times I held on tight and came up on the skis, only to topple over and fall face down back into the water. The fourth attempt was a little better, and I actually managed to get up and into the crouch for a few seconds before toppling over, and this is my fifth, and final, attempt before Ed has a go.

I run through the checklist they've been teaching me. Skis pointing up – check. Legs bent into my chest – check. Arms straight out – check. The boat passes by slowly with the rope trailing behind it, and I grab the handle as it comes past, making sure the rope is now running straight between my skis.

'Go!' I shout, and tense my body in preparation for the pull on the rope. As it comes, I'm ready for it. I keep my legs bent as the rope pulls me out of the water, and lean back a little as I come into the crouch. Incredibly, I'm up and I don't feel like I'm about to fall. Tentatively, I start to straighten my legs as the boat begins to turn out into the bay. I keep my eyes up, looking where I'm going. I'm standing now, and it feels amazing! I can see Ed in the boat, taking pictures on my camera, and I give him a wave.

That proves to be my undoing. As soon as I let go of the handle with one hand, my balance goes and I crash into the water again. I don't mind though. I'm beaming from ear to ear as the boat circles back to pick me up.

'That was brilliant, Charley! Well done! I hope I got some decent pictures, particularly of the last one.'

'That was so much fun!' I enthuse as we head back into the shallows so that Ed can have his turn. He shows me how to take pictures and video on his phone, before climbing into the water.

It turns out that Ed has neglected to tell me something, which is that he has done this before. He's a little rusty, so his first attempt ends in failure, but on the second he rises up smoothly and is soon standing and weaving from one side of the boat to the other through the waves as we head out in a wide circle around the bay. I have to admit I'm impressed, and after a while I put my camera and the phone down and just enjoy watching him. As his time draws to a close, we head back towards the shore. At the last minute the boat turns to avoid running aground, and he lets go of the rope and sinks gracefully back into the water near the beach.

'You never told me you could ski! That was awesome!' I tell him as soon as we're both back on dry land.

'Well, I haven't done it for a while, but I used to enjoy it when I was growing up. There was this big lake near where we lived, and I used to go down there as often as I could to ski. I'd forgotten how much fun it was. I have to say doing it here, with warm water and sunshine, beats the hell out of doing it on a cold lake in England!'

'Is this how it's going to be with all the activities?' I ask him. 'Are you secretly an Olympic windsurfer? Maybe you've kayaked down the Amazon?'

He laughs. 'I promise I've never windsurfed in my life and, although we did do some kayaking at school, it's not exactly hard so I don't think you're going to struggle there. You were excellent for a first-time skier though. That last one was superb!'

'Yeah, shame I got distracted by a cute boy in the boat,' I reply, nudging him in the ribs.

'Cute, eh? I can live with that.'

At dinner, Ed relates our afternoon adventures to my parents and insists on showing them the video of my last run. I notice that he glosses over my first few attempts. I watch him as he talks. His face is bright with enthusiasm and his eyes are sparkling. Stupid Sarah, I find myself thinking. She has no idea what she's missed out on.

Mum and Dad are suitably impressed by the footage. 'I had a go once, a few years ago,' Dad admits. 'I couldn't get on with it at all.'

'You should have seen Ed, Dad. He's a pro!' I squeeze Ed's hand proudly as I speak, and I feel him squeeze mine back.

'What are you up to tomorrow?' Dad asks.

'Windsurfing and kayaking. Apparently, there's a little beach on the other side of the bay that's quite nice, so we thought we might go and check that out for a change of scenery.'

I feel the first twinges of stiffness across my shoulders and down my legs as I get ready for bed that night. It looks like I'm going to be sore tomorrow, but I don't care. I've had a blast today doing something that I've never done before, and I'm looking forward to more of the same over the next few days.

As I drift off to sleep, images of the day play through my mind. I'm so glad I came on this holiday, and I'm glad to have met Ed. As I think about him, I'm aware of butterflies fluttering deep in my stomach.

'Are you falling for him, Charley?' I ask myself out loud.

'I think I might be, just a little,' I reply.

I turn over and, within moments, I'm fast asleep.

15

When I wake up, I'm delighted to discover that, although I am a bit stiff, it's nowhere near as bad as it could have been. I had been worried that I'd have to pass on the windsurfing due to my muscles being on strike, but I reckon I'll be OK as long as I don't overdo it.

I look at the bedside clock, which tells me it's eight thirty already and I've missed having breakfast with my parents. I'm not due to meet Ed until ten, so I have a leisurely shower and then wander up to the restaurant for breakfast. On the way back to my room I finally remember to pick up some earplugs; although I haven't had any repeat performances from my parents, I don't want to be caught out again.

Ed is waiting for me as I approach the water sports hut, and my heart quickens slightly when I see him. 'For God's sake, Charley, get a grip,' I tell myself sternly, but it doesn't make any difference.

'How are you this morning?' he asks with a smile. 'Not too stiff, I hope?'

'I'm a little sore,' I confess, 'but I'm looking forward to this too much to let a little stiffness get in the way.'

We put on our life jackets and walk out to where the wind-surf boards are. While we're still on the beach, the instructor teaches us how to position our bodies, and raise and hold the sail. To be honest, it seems pretty straightforward and, after a couple of practices, we head out into the water to try it for real.

If I thought water-skiing was hard, this is in a whole new league. Once you've got onto the board, you've got to try to keep your balance while you try to pull the sail out of the water. This is next to impossible, and both Ed and I fall in several times. The problem is that the sail is really heavy when it's lying down because it's full of water so, if you're not careful, you overbalance and fall in on top of it. Then if you avoid that, as it comes up and the water runs out of it, it suddenly becomes much lighter and, if you're not ready for that, you tip off the board backwards.

'This is impossible!' Ed exclaims after falling in the water for the umpteenth time.

'Now you know how I felt yesterday. At least we're on a level playing field this time,' I reply with a smile.

'I think these boards are sabotaged,' he splutters as he surfaces following his latest disastrous attempt.

I can't help but laugh, which proves to be unwise as I promptly lose my footing, fall in face first and end up swallowing yet another mouthful of salty water. Once I surface, I can see Ed's desperately trying not to repeat my experience. It's been like this all morning, we're completely in sync.

'Sabotaged or not,' I tell him, as I clamber back onto mine,

'I'm determined not to let it win. It can't be as impossible as it feels, otherwise nobody would do it. Come on, we'll get there.'

He lets out a small sigh and climbs back on.

After several more attempts, both Ed and I manage to get the sail out of the water without falling off. Neither of us look elegant, and I can feel my legs shaking with the strain of trying to keep my balance, but we're up and the first battle is over. The instructor reminds us how to position ourselves and hold the boom to angle the sail into the breeze and, after another couple of falls, we tentatively set off.

By the end of the lesson, the muscles in my arms and legs are begging for mercy, but I've managed to sail from one end of the beach to the other, turn around and sail back again, all without falling off. Poor Ed is not quite so lucky, but only because he fell off during the turn.

'That was really hard,' Ed remarks as we walk up to get some lunch. 'I'm definitely going to pay for that later. I've worked muscles I never knew I had!'

'I think we were beginning to get the hang of it by the end though,' I reply. 'A few more lessons and I might actually be able to do it without looking like I'm hanging on for dear life.'

'Are you sure you're up to kayaking this afternoon?' Ed asks. 'It is much gentler and we can go slowly, but if you'd rather just lie on the beach and recover, I quite understand.'

'I think that we'd better do it while we can still move,' I reply. 'If we leave it until tomorrow, we might find we're not up to it!'

After lunch, we go back to the water sports hut and get our kayaks. Ed is right, this is much easier, and I love the restful sloshing sound of the water against the bow as I paddle across the bay. Ed is alongside me as we head for the beach that we've been told about. When we get there, we pull the kayaks up onto the sand and Ed produces two towels from his and spreads them out for us to lie on. There are a few other people dotted about, but it's much quieter than the hotel beach. I remove my life jacket and lie down on the towel. Ed flops down beside me.

'So, one of the exercises the other couples in the programme will be doing around now is a questionnaire, apparently. Do you know about this?' Ed asks.

Since our first conversation, Ed has realised that I'm quite an expert when it comes to *Married Before We Met*. 'Oh, yes. It usually ends in one of them revealing something that is going to be a massive problem for the other person, and then there are loads of trust issues that have to be worked through,' I reply.

'I've got the one that Sarah and I were supposed to be doing. I thought it might be something fun for us to have a go at before we paddle back, but if it's going to open a can of worms then perhaps I'll leave it.'

'No. Go on. I don't think I have anything to hide, do you?'

'I don't think so. OK, let's do the first couple of questions and, if we don't like it, we'll stop there. What do you think?'

I sit up on the towel, turn towards him and cross my legs. He does the same so we're facing each other.

'OK. Question one. How many sexual partners have you had?'

'Wow, they don't mess about, do they? Straight for the

jugular!' I laugh. 'OK, fine. I've had two. The first one was called Darren, who I've recently learned is gay, and then there was Josh. You?'

'Also two,' he replies. 'I was a late starter. I went to an all-boys school, so I didn't know any girls until university, where I met this girl called Nicola. She was the polar opposite of me. She was this wild, unpredictable, hippy-type creature and I was mesmerised by her. We went out for most of the time we were studying, but it came to a fairly natural end in the final year as we knew we were headed in different directions. We kept in vague touch for a couple of years, but even that fizzled out eventually.'

'And the other?'

'Office romance. A colleague of mine, in the early days. It didn't last very long. I think we were both a bit overwhelmed by the pressures of working in a big law firm, and used each other as a bit of a comfort blanket. Once we got more confident, we realised we weren't really compatible and ended it. I'm still friends with her. She works at a different firm now and is married with two children.

'OK. I think that's question one finished,' Ed continues. 'How are you feeling? Are you happy to carry on?'

'I'm fine so far if you are. Let's have the next one,' I reply.

'This is a two-parter. Have you ever cheated on a partner, and have you ever been cheated on by a partner?'

'I've never cheated, no,' I answer. 'Although both my relationships ended because my partner was cheating on me. Darren was getting blow jobs from another girl in my year, and Josh and Scarlett you know about already. Actually, now I come to think about it, that's not a great track record for me, is it? Maybe there's something about me that drives boyfriends into the arms of other women. Maybe I'm shit at sex or something, and they didn't bother to tell me, they just went and got it elsewhere.'

Ed is obviously aware that I'm building myself up into a fit of insecurity and intervenes. 'I think that's unlikely. Sex is a two-way street. If there was an issue, and I'm sure there wasn't, it was just as much their fault for not taking time to find out what you like. In my opinion the issue here is simple.'

'Oh yes?'

'They're dickheads.'

I burst out laughing. 'OK. Enough of my insecurities then. What about you?'

'No. I've never cheated. The answer to the second question is rather more difficult though. I'm going to have to answer that I'm not sure whether I've been cheated on or not.'

'Go on.' This sounds interesting.

'As I said before, Nicola was something of a free spirit, and never made any bones about the fact that she also found women attractive. I'm pretty sure she never cheated on me with another man, but I had my suspicions about whether she was closer to one or two of her female friends than she let on.'

'She sounds quite a character. What's question three?'

'Do you want children? If so, how many? It says here that if either party already has children this should be interpreted as "do you want any more".'

'Yes, definitely. I'm not in a blinding rush though. My biological clock is not screaming at me to get on with it. I'd want to be married first – I'm traditional like that – but after that, yes. You?'

'Yes. Now that I've climbed high enough up the greasy pole that I don't have to be working every hour of every day, I think I'm probably ready. I couldn't be one of those absentee fathers who only see their children for a few hours at the weekend. I'd want to be around and involved in their lives.'

I study him. 'I reckon you'd make a good dad,' I tell him.

He looks surprised but flattered. 'Thanks. I'm sure you'll be a great mother when the time comes.'

Question four is where I finally come undone. It tells us to look at our partner and tell them five things we love about them. Although I can think of several things I love about Ed, we're not in that type of relationship and I'm far too embarrassed. Thankfully, it appears that he feels the same and doesn't insist. As the sun starts to dip, we get back into the kayaks and paddle back to the main beach.

'I'm really feeling the strain of this morning,' I say to Ed when we get back. 'I'm going to have a hot bath and I'll see you at the bar at the usual time, OK?'

'Actually, and I hope you don't mind, but I've arranged something slightly different for this evening. Are you OK to meet me a little earlier?'

I'm intrigued and we agree to meet at six thirty. When I get back to my room, I run a bath as hot as I can bear and lower myself into it, letting the heat from the water soothe my aching muscles. Once I've dried myself off, I take a little bit of extra care over my appearance before I set off to meet Ed at the bar.

As usual he's waiting for me but, instead of ordering a drink, he takes my hand and starts to lead me away.

'Where are we going?' I ask him. I'm very conscious of his hand around mine. It's a nice sensation.

'Wait and see!' As we make our way through the grounds, it dawns on me where he's taking me.

'Ed, are we going to your room?'

He obviously senses my uncertainty because he stops, lets go of my hand, and turns to face me.

'It's nothing pervy, I promise. It's just that you seemed so keen on the picnic, so I started wondering what I could do that was similar. The hotel does offer dinner on the beach, but they have quite a few tables set up and it didn't feel very exclusive, so I've asked them to lay on something special on my balcony instead. The view might not be breathtaking, but it's pretty good.'

'Oh, Ed. What a lovely idea. Is that what you were doing at reception yesterday when you said you'd forgotten something?'

He has the decency to blush slightly. 'It might be.'

'But what about Mum and Dad? They might be worried if we don't turn up for dinner with them.'

'I spoke to them at breakfast this morning and told them that I'd planned a surprise for you. Your mother was absolutely delighted.'

'Oh God, I bet she was. She's probably searching the internet for wedding hats as we speak!'

Ed's face falls slightly. 'I didn't think of that. Sorry. Would you rather we abandon this plan and go and join them? I don't want to give your mother the wrong impression.'

I take a moment to think about it. Although I'm slightly uncomfortable about going to his room, I'm pretty sure he's not an axe murderer and he's obviously gone to a lot of trouble to organise this dinner for me. I'm also more than a little curious to see what the honeymoon suite looks like, as I've never been in one before.

I take his hand again. 'I think it's a lovely plan, Ed. Thank you. Show me the way.'

16

The honeymoon suite is enormous! When Ed opens the door and stands aside for me to go in, I find myself in a large sitting room. There are two very comfortable-looking sofas, a fully stocked bar with a refrigerator underneath, an upmarket stereo system and a huge flat-screen TV. The fans on the ceiling are turning silently and lazily, creating the slightest movement of the air-conditioned air. Off to the left is a door that I imagine must lead into the bedroom.

'Wow! This is a bit of an upgrade from my room. Is it OK if I look around?' I ask Ed.

'Be my guest. What can I get you to drink? I've got rum and Coke if you fancy it?'

'That sounds perfect. Thank you.'

I open the door and walk into the bedroom. It's dominated by the biggest four-poster bed I think I've ever clapped eyes on. It's modern and similar in style to the one in my room, but must be nearly twice the size.

'I thought the idea of a honeymoon was that you were

close together,' I call to Ed in the next room. 'This bed is so big you're practically in different time zones!'

'I know. It's ridiculous, isn't it?' he calls back. 'I've done some tests, and I reckon you could lie one person on each side, they could both spread their arms and legs as wide as they possibly could, and they still wouldn't be touching each other.'

I look around at the rest of the room. It's very tidy – Ed is obviously not a 'floordrobe' man. There's a slight hint of his aftershave in the air and I spot the bottle on the dressing table. I pick it up and read the label. It's Penhaligon's. Not a brand I've heard of. I spray a little bit just in front of my nose and sniff it. It really is very nice.

I walk back out into the living area and Ed hands me my drink. 'The bathroom is through there,' he says, pointing at another door. 'If you thought the bed was ridiculous, you really ought to check that out.'

He's right. It's another huge room, pretty much covered from floor to ceiling with marble. On one wall there's a walk-in shower with not only a rainfall showerhead, but those little jets that squirt you from lots of other angles too. Opposite the shower there is an enormous mirror, with his and hers basins underneath.

In the centre of the room there are two large baths, arranged head-to-toe. Between them is a shelf with candles.

'Check this out!' calls Ed from the other room. Suddenly soft music fills the bathroom, I look around but can't spot the speakers.

He sticks his head around the door. 'The lights are dimmable, so you can light the candles, put some music on, fill a bath or two and have a drink. They've thought of everything. I have to say it's a bit of a step up from the bathroom in my flat, and I've got serious shower envy. You haven't seen the best bit yet, though.'

He takes my hand again and leads me out onto the balcony. He's right. The view is great. It looks straight out over the bay to the sea beyond. I can see various boats out there, their lights twinkling in the falling darkness. Above them hangs the moon, casting its light onto the ocean and making it glitter. On the beach below I can see the tables that Ed mentioned before. A few of them are already occupied and waiters are moving around serving food and drinks. Each table is in its own little bubble of light, created by the candles in the middle. The air is thick with the sound of cicadas, and I lean on the railing, letting the warm breeze wash over me as I sip my drink and listen. I'm aware of Ed standing next to me, but he doesn't speak.

'This is lovely,' I murmur after a while.

'It's not too shabby, is it?' Ed replies. 'They'll bring our first course at seven thirty. I hope you don't mind, but I kind of had to choose what we wanted when I booked it, so I hope I've ordered things you like.'

I turn around and see that a table has been set up with two chairs, flowers and candles in glass holders. Next to the table are two ice buckets. One contains a bottle of champagne and the other a bottle of white wine. I spot a bottle of red on the table as well.

'We're going to be totally plastered if we drink all of that!' I say to Ed.

'I wasn't sure what you'd be in the mood for, so I thought I'd better cover all the bases,' he replies. 'Would you like to stay out here until the food comes, or would you be happier inside?'

'Out here, definitely. It's just so beautiful. Thank you so much, Ed, for organising this. It's the nicest thing anyone has done for me in ages.' I walk over to him and give him a kiss on the cheek, before settling myself at the table.

'You mean, besides the whole "free holiday in Antigua" thing that your parents did?'

I laugh. 'Yes, besides that I suppose.'

At seven thirty there's a knock on the door and Ed goes to open it. A waiter appears with a trolley and two plates covered with cloches. He silently places them on the table, lifts off the cloches with a dramatic flourish, and then leaves, shutting the door behind him.

'Smoked salmon, prawn and cucumber mousse, served with lemon, shell-on prawns and salmon caviar,' Ed announces, reading off the menu. 'Does that sound OK?'

My stomach is rumbling in anticipation. 'That sounds fabulous. Thank you.'

'And what would you like to drink?'

'I think, as you've gone to all this trouble, it would be rude not to have a small glass of champagne, don't you?'

Ed smiles and adopts a French accent 'An egg-zellent choice, mademoiselle. *Permettez-moi.* I mean, allow me.'

He busies himself with the bottle, and I watch him. He's obviously done this a few times before as the foil and wire cage are off in moments, and he pops the cork without spilling a drop. He pours some out for each of us and we start to eat.

The mousse is the most delicious thing I think I've ever eaten. It's light, but you can taste all the main ingredients, and it goes beautifully with the champagne. I'm a little daunted by the prawns, so Ed takes them and shells them for me, before passing them back. I notice we each have little finger bowls with tiny towels next to them for cleaning our hands. They really have thought of everything.

Some time after we've finished our starters, the waiter appears again. He takes away all the debris and places two new plates in front of us. Once again, the cloches are removed with a little flourish. Once again, Ed reads from the menu.

'Cannon of lamb glazed with rosemary and mustard, served with Parmentier potatoes, roasted vegetables and a red wine jus.'

It smells amazing. 'I hate to be wasteful,' I say to Ed, 'but I think I'd like to change to a little bit of red wine to go with this.'

'Good idea,' he replies. He takes my half-empty champagne glass and places it on the side, replacing it with a fresh one into which he pours some red wine, and then repeats the process for himself. The lamb is beautifully tender, and I sigh with pleasure as I bite into it. The wine is big and bold, and goes very nicely with the lamb. I make sure I'm only having small sips as I don't want to get drunk. I want to savour, and remember, every moment of this beautiful evening.

As we eat and drink, we talk about our childhoods. I learn that Ed grew up in Somerset, where his parents have a large house with substantial gardens. His father was a corporate lawyer and made a lot of money before retiring early 'while I'm still young enough to enjoy it'. There was never any pressure from his father for Ed to follow in his footsteps, but Ed found he was interested in the law, so decided to make a career out of it like his father had. I can sense his admiration for his father, but I get the impression that they're not particularly close. He's obviously devoted to his mother, though. Both he and his sister went to boarding schools, but their mum used to send regular food parcels, and would make sure that she cooked their favourite foods on the night they got home at the end of each term.

I tell him about growing up, about school, and how our lives changed as my father's business got more successful. He asks about Simon, Emma and the girls, and I tell him about the puppy, and how Emma and my mum are thick as thieves.

'Does that bother you? Do you feel like she's edging you out?'

'No, not at all. I love her to bits. She's one of those people who it's almost impossible not to like. Plus, she's been around for so long she's practically a sister to me.'

I tell him about Mads. 'She sounds like a feisty woman,' he remarks. 'I wouldn't want to be on the wrong side of her!'

'She is a force of nature, certainly, but she's incredibly kind in her rather direct, no-nonsense way. Sometimes I want to kill her, but she's my best friend and I know she's got my back.'

When the waiter reappears with our puddings a while later, it's so obvious what they are when the cloches come off that I don't need Ed to read off the menu again.

'Chocolate fondant!' I exclaim. 'I bloody love this!'

I press my spoon into the sponge and, as I cut it in two, the filling oozes out. It's rich and smooth, especially when I add a little bit of cream from the jug on the table.

'Mmm, God, that's good!' I exclaim, with my mouth full.

Ed looks at me and laughs. 'I don't think I've ever met a woman who enjoys her food as much as you do!'

'Ah well, if you could see what I was forced to live on for the last couple of years with Josh, you'd understand.'

When we've finished, I retrieve the glass of champagne and go back to leaning on the balcony rail. The alcohol has softened everything nicely, but I'm still in full control of myself. I look down at the tables on the beach. Most of them are occupied now, and the waiters are working hard. Ed comes and stands next to me again. Automatically I reach out my hand and take his. We stand there for a long time in silence.

Eventually, I turn to him. 'That was amazing, thank you so much. It was a lovely idea and everything was just perfect. Total high point of my holiday so far!'

He turns to me, and he has a slight frown. 'What?' I ask. Maybe he thinks I'm coming on too strong.

'You have a little smear of chocolate,' he remarks. 'May I?'

I nod, and he reaches out and wipes his thumb across my bottom lip. As he does so, I kiss it lightly and lift my eyes to his. Time seems to stand still for a moment, then he gently cups my face in his hands and lowers his lips onto mine.

The kiss is soft, like a question. I wrap my arms around him and the kiss deepens. I respond to him and press myself against him, kissing him harder. My hand wraps round the back of his head and I curl my fingers into his hair. He pulls me into him, wrapping his arm around me, and I lose myself in the kiss and the smell of him. After what feels like an age, we gently pull apart.

'Shall we continue this inside?' he asks, and I nod.

As we go into the bedroom, the atmosphere between us shifts. The presence of the bed makes what we are about to do feel much more real somehow, and I'm suddenly a bit anxious. I'm used to the familiarity of sex with Josh, but Ed is unfamiliar and new. What if I really am no good at it? I don't want to disappoint Ed, but the certainty I felt out on the balcony has deserted me.

Ed picks up my reticence. 'Are you OK? We don't have to...'

'No, I want to,' I reply. 'It's just that I'm a bit nervous, I suppose.'

'I tell you what. Let's just cuddle up together and have a bit of a kiss. If it develops into more then that's fine, and if it doesn't, well, that's also fine. OK?'

I nod, and he leads me over to the bed. We lie down together and I nestle into him, wrapping my arms around him. He kisses my hair, and I turn my face up and kiss him on the lips. We stay like that for a while, just holding each other and kissing gently, and I feel my nervousness begin to subside. I run my hands over his shirt, feeling the unfamiliar contours of his body beneath. I look at his face, and the kindness in his eyes as he looks back at me. He really is a good man, and if anyone is going to be the one to 'get me back on the horse', as Mads would put it, I want it to be him. He gently strokes his hand down my neck and onto my shoulder.

'Is this OK?' he asks, as he begins to move his hand lower. I nod, and he gently brushes over my breast and down onto my stomach. He leans in and kisses me again, still gently. I can feel my body beginning to respond to him, and I reach down and carefully guide his hand back onto my breast. We continue kissing as he gently cups and squeezes it through the fabric of my top and bra.

'Why don't you take off your shirt?' I suggest, after a while.

He disentangles himself from me and takes it off, dumping it on the floor by the bed. As he lies down again, I lean back slightly to study him. Although I've seen his chest before, I've never really looked at it in the way that I am now. It's hairy enough to be masculine, without being over the top. I reach out and put my hand on it, running my fingers through the hair. I kiss him again, and my resolve strengthens. I sit up and pull my top over my head, sending it to join his shirt on the floor, before lying back down next to him. He traces the line of my shoulder with his finger and runs it down my arm, before coming back up my stomach and onto my breast once more.

'God, you're beautiful,' he murmurs. He reaches round behind me to undo my bra strap. 'May I?' he asks, and I nod once more. As soon as it's off he pulls me into him and kisses me deeply. My desire builds as my final reservations fall away.

I push him onto his back and straddle him. I now know without any doubt where I want this to go.

* * *

Some time later, we're lying together in silence, our limbs entwined. Sex with Ed was satisfying and exciting in a way that I'd forgotten existed, and I've realised how lazy and stuck in a rut Josh and I had become. I'm stroking his hair gently and he's running a finger lazily up and down my arm. After a while, a thought comes to me and I giggle.

'What?' he asks.

I glance down at our naked bodies. 'I don't think the couple's massage is going to pose any intimacy problems now, is it?'

'Just as well!' He laughs. 'After all the exertion, both today and this evening, I think we might need it!

'Charley,' he asks after a while, 'I don't want to get all heavy and start a conversation about "us", but where do you think we go from here? I'm not a "fling" sort of person, I don't want you to think that I'm going to drop you like a hot potato now that I've had my wicked way with you. Maybe, when we get back to England...'

I put my finger on his lips to shush him. 'Let's not make any promises we don't know we can keep. I'm not a fling person either, but England seems like a different world at the moment. Why don't we enjoy what we have while we can and just see what happens?'

He nods and I give him a long kiss. 'Do you know what I'd enjoy right now?' I ask him.

'I don't think I'm ready for another round just yet!' He looks alarmed.

'I wasn't going to say that, actually!' I laugh. 'What I'd enjoy right now is another glass of champagne, if there's any left.'

'Hang on, I'll be right back.'

He leaves the room and reappears moments later with two very fluffy white dressing gowns. He puts one on and hands the other to me. I put it on and follow him back out onto the balcony, where he refills our glasses. The detritus of our dinner is still on the table.

'Shit!' I exclaim. 'You don't think they tried to come and clear up while we, you know...?'

'No.' He laughs. 'After they've served the final course, they leave it and I think the cleaners probably take it when they come in the morning.'

We sit in silence for a while, sipping our champagne. The beach is in complete darkness now, and the only lights come from the moon and the downlighters illuminating the paths. The last few guests are making their way back to their rooms from whatever evening entertainment has been laid on. The air feels heavy, and soon the first fat raindrops start to fall.

'Time to beat a retreat, I think,' Ed says. 'When it rains here, it really throws it down.'

He's not wrong. He dims the lights once we're inside, and we watch through the window as a storm of biblical proportions comes in from the sea. The rain falls in curtains, and there is thunder and lightning overhead.

'I love watching lightning,' I say. 'It's like Mother Nature is reminding us who's really in charge. When I was small, I'd always open my curtains and watch if there was a thunder-storm. I used to enjoy counting the time between seeing the flash and hearing the thunder, to try to work out how far away it was. I still do, actually.'

'You know what this means though?' Ed replies. 'It means you're stuck here with me for the night. Unless you fancy getting soaked and want to take the risk of being struck by lightning on your way back?'

I snuggle into him. 'I can think of worse places to be. Just make sure you wake me up and boot me out early enough in the morning so that I can get back to my room before Mum and Dad notice I'm not there. The last thing we need is them on our case.'

'Deal,' he replies. 'What about the massage? Shall I ring and book us in?'

'Yes, that sounds like an excellent idea.'

Ed crosses to the phone and rings reception. After a short conversation, he comes back and sits down next to me. 'They had a slot at ten in the morning, so I booked that. I hope that's OK?'

We finish our champagne and head back into the bedroom. I climb in under the covers and we lie there, facing each other. I pull him close for a hug and feel something pressing into me.

'I see you've recovered.' I smile as I reach down and stroke him softly. 'It would be a shame to waste it.'

He rolls me onto my back and starts kissing his way down my neck again.

'My thoughts exactly.'

18

Ed is as good as his word, and I find myself doing the walk of shame at seven the next morning. I say walk, but it's more of a hobble. The muscles in my arms and legs are protesting wildly with every step, but I'm still smiling from the memories of the evening before. There's no sign of my parents as I slot the key in and open the door to my room as quietly as I can. Once I'm inside, I quickly draw the curtains to make it look as if I've been there all night. I'd love to soak in a bath to soothe my aching limbs, but I don't have time for that if I'm going to have breakfast with Mum and Dad, so I quickly strip off and step into the shower.

There is the faintest whiff of Ed's aftershave hanging in the room as I come out of the shower, which I trace to the top I was wearing last night. I can't help myself; I pick it up and breathe in deeply, causing flutters to ripple through my stomach. By eight, I'm washed, dressed and ready to go.

'Good grief, Charlotte, what on earth have you done to

yourself?' my mother exclaims as I limp after them towards the restaurant.

'I think I've overdone it with water-skiing and windsurfing, that's all,' I reply. 'I'm going to have a massage a bit later, which will hopefully help, and then I'm probably going to lie on the beach and take it easy today. Give my body a chance to recover.'

'And how was your evening last night? Ed said he'd planned a surprise for you. Was it nice?'

What to say? If I tell them I was in his room, Mum will draw all sorts of (correct) conclusions that I don't want her to, but if I invent something it might all unravel later and catch me out. I decide to tell the truth, but leave out some of the details, such as the fact that I was in his room. Oh, and the fact that we had sex, obviously.

'It was lovely. Ed arranged a special dinner for me because one of the experiences from his honeymoon that I wanted to try was the picnic, but that's arranged by the production company so we couldn't do it. The dinner was his idea of a substitute.' I fill her in on the details of what we ate and drank, but carefully leave out the location.

'I hope you managed to get back before the storm came in,' Dad says. 'That was quite something.'

'Yes, I was safely tucked up in bed, thank goodness.' Just not in my bed.

After breakfast, I go back to Ed's room and sit on the balcony while he finishes getting ready. He's just as sore as me, so we stagger together down to the spa for our massage.

'Goodness me, what have you two been up to?' the therapist asks as we arrive. Once we've explained, she goes to get her colleague and I hear them chatting in low voices.

'OK,' she says when they both return, 'I'm Barbara and this is my colleague, Ruby, and we'll be doing your couple's massage today. Normally the couple's massage is an aromatherapy massage. It does help to relax your muscles and joints, but we've just been having a chat and we think you two would actually benefit more from a sports massage. It's a bit more intense than the aromatherapy massage, but it will do you more good. What do you say?'

We agree, and they lead us to the treatment room where there are two massage beds laid out next to each other.

'We'll leave you here to get ready,' Barbara explains. 'You just need to strip down to your underwear – you can leave your clothes on the chairs there – and lie face down on the beds. There's a little towel on each bed to cover yourself with, and you can see a hole that you can stick your face into to be more comfortable. Charlotte, you'll need to remove your bra, if that's OK.'

They retreat and Ed and I start to undress. Even after everything we did together last night, it still seems slightly awkward to be undressing in front of him, and I can see he's having a slight arousal issue as I take off my bra and put it with my other clothes.

'Stop looking at me,' I tell him, 'and think about your great-aunt Mildred instead.'

'I don't have a great-aunt Mildred!' he replies.

'Oh yes you do,' I tell him as I climb onto the bed and cover myself with the towel. 'She's old, and fat, and she has a hairy wart on the end of her nose. She smells of cats, and not in a good way, and you can feel the hairs from her wart tickling you as she presses you into her enormous bosom. Picture it, and breathe in the strange cat smell.'

'OK, thank you. Crisis averted.' He climbs onto his bed and covers himself.

After a little while there's a knock on the door. 'Are you ready?' asks Barbara's voice from the other side.

'Yes,' we reply and they come in. Soft music starts playing.

'We're going to use black pepper oil,' Barbara explains. 'It's warming, and really good for tired, stiff muscles. Now, as I explained to you earlier, this is a bit more intense than the aromatherapy massage, and it might even hurt a bit, but you'll really feel the difference afterwards.'

The first part of the massage is fairly gentle, but then as the hour progresses it ramps up in intensity until we're being kneaded and pounded. It gets to the point where I'm sure it's actually more painful than the original stiff muscles were and, if I were capable of speech beyond the occasional exclamation of 'Oof' and 'Bloody hell', I'd make a wisecrack about the cure being worse than the disease. At one point, Ed turns his face to me and says, 'This is extra, you know. We're actually paying these very kind ladies to hurt us. Is that a bit weird?' before crying out as Ruby digs her elbow into his shoulder and pulls back on his arm.

Afterwards, they leave us to get dressed, and then guide us to two very comfortable-looking reclining chairs, each with a bottle of water in a holder in the armrest.

'Stay here for as long as you like,' Barbara tells us. 'Make sure you drink plenty of water today, and take it easy. By tomorrow you'll be feeling like new people.'

We stay for a while and finish the bottles of water they've provided, and then wander back to Ed's room. I'm still sore, but I can feel my muscles have relaxed a bit and I'm able to walk fairly normally. Ed also seems much improved.

When we get back, we fill up the head-to-toe baths in his suite and peel off our clothes. I climb into one of them and lie back, closing my eyes and letting the hot water continue the good work the therapist did earlier. After a while, I open them and look at Ed in the other bath. 'You know what we're missing here?' I ask him.

'Champagne?' he replies. 'I've got a tiny bottle in the mini-bar. Probably enough for a glass each.'

'Perfect,' I tell him.

He gets out of the bath and dries himself off a bit before heading into the sitting room to fetch the drinks. After a minute or so, he returns and places two glasses on the shelf between the baths.

I top up my bath with some more hot water and then take a sip of cold champagne. 'That's much better,' I say to Ed, and we chink glasses.

Once the champagne is gone and the heat has started to go out of the water, we dry ourselves off and get dressed. Ed orders lunch from room service, and we sit out on the balcony to eat it. We then spend a lazy afternoon on the beach, until it's time to get ready to meet Mum and Dad at the bar.

'Charlotte tells me you two have been putting each other through the mill,' my dad remarks to Ed over dinner. 'She was quite sore this morning.'

Ed nearly spits out his drink and I hastily intervene. 'I think water-skiing and windsurfing on consecutive days was probably a bit much, but we had a sports massage earlier, and it's really helped.'

'Were you massaged together?' my mum asks, fixing me with a beady stare.

'Yes, but Ed was a perfect gentleman and turned his back when I got changed,' I lie. I'm not sure she's buying it, but she doesn't say any more and the conversation moves on to safer ground.

After dinner, Mum and Dad announce that they're going to head back to the bar for a nightcap. Ed and I plead tiredness and retreat to his room, where we climb into bed and make love before curling up and falling fast asleep.

The next morning we're up early for our jeep tour. The sports massage has worked miracles and most of the aches and pains have gone. I dash back to my room to have a quick shower and get changed before meeting Ed back at reception where our driver, Steve, is waiting for us.

The tour is fascinating. Steve turns out to be a mine of information about Antigua and its politics. He tells us how the island's economy used to be based entirely on sugar, and about the life of slaves on the sugar plantations. We visit Betty's Hope, where the windmill that was used to crush the sugar cane to extract the juice has been restored. He takes us on to the Devil's Bridge, a natural rock arch formed by years of the Atlantic Ocean crashing against it, and explains how slaves used to cross the bridge and drown themselves to escape their captors. Ed and I are a bit quiet after that; there's something disconcerting about being on this paradise island and coming face to face with its dark past. As we trundle along the roads, I look out of the window at the people going about their business and reflect on the fact that most of their ancestors were brought here against their will and treated with appalling cruelty. I'm still thinking about it when we stop at a roadside shack and taste a variety of fruit. We continue on to English Harbour for a tour of Nelson's dockyard and take photos of ourselves with the red phone box, which lightens the mood.

After lunch, Steve takes us up to Shirley Heights for a different view of the dockyard, before driving us back to the hotel. A rain shower passes over as we drive back, and Steve has to slow right down as it's difficult to see. Ed and I hold hands in the back of the jeep, and I lean across and rest my head on his shoulder.

By the time we get back to the hotel, the rain has cleared and the paths are steaming as the water evaporates under the sunlight. We get changed and head for the beach.

'You seem a little subdued this afternoon. Are you still thinking about what Steve told us about the slave trade here?' I ask Ed once we've settled ourselves on the reserved sunloungers.

'A little, but mainly I'm just thinking about going home tomorrow. I'm going to miss you,' he replies.

'I'm going to miss you too,' I tell him. 'But your flight isn't until the evening, so we've got the rest of today and most of tomorrow. Let's try to make the most of them. Come on, I'll race you into the sea.'

We charge into the sea together and, once the water is getting too deep for me to stand, I wrap my arms around Ed's shoulders, my legs around his waist and kiss him. 'I feel so lucky to have met you,' I tell him.

'Me too,' he replies.

I study his face. I think I might be falling in love with him, but I'm too scared to say it out loud. What I do know is that it feels like I've known him for a lot longer than just a few days. I rest my head on his shoulder. I don't want this to end any more than he does, but I'm determined to be realistic. We live very different lives back in the UK, and the connection we've made in this little holiday bubble may not be strong enough to translate back home.

As the sun starts to dip in the sky, we head back to his room to make love, before separating to get ready for dinner. The evening follows its usual format; we meet Mum and Dad in the bar for a drink, then go to eat together. Tonight, as it's Ed's last night, Dad has booked the pan-Asian restaurant. I still think it's incongruous in this setting, but there's no doubting the deliciousness of the food. Ed's mood seems to have recovered and he regales Mum and Dad with anonymised stories of some of his more outrageous clients. Every so often he catches my eye and smiles at me. I smile back.

I'm definitely falling in love with him.

19

We're awoken the next morning by a pounding on the door. Ed sits bolt upright.

'Oh, fuck!' he exclaims. 'Fuck, fuck, fuck!' He leaps out of bed and starts throwing on clothes.

'What is it? What's the matter?'

'It's the bloody camera crew. They've come to do a final interview with me before I go home, and I completely forgot about it. If they see you, they'll be all over you like a pack of hyenas. I don't want that for you. I agreed to this. You didn't.'

I can see him trying to work out what to do as he pulls on his trousers and slips his feet into his shoes. There's another pounding on the door and he sticks his head out of the bedroom and shouts, 'I'M COMING – GIVE ME FIVE MINUTES,' at the main door.

'This will take an hour at the most,' he says. 'Are you OK to stay in here while I do this interview and I'll come and get you once they're gone?'

I consider my options. My only escape route is out of the

main door, which will put me straight in their path, so it seems I don't really have a choice.

'Yes, fine.'

He closes the bedroom door behind him, and I listen to him admitting the camera crew. There's a guy called Dave, who seems to be in charge, and Jamie, who is obviously his sidekick. The bedroom door is not thick, and I can hear most of what they're saying through it. There's a certain amount of faffing about while they get their equipment set up and get the sound levels right, and then the interview commences.

'So, Ed. In your own words, tell us what you've been doing since you got here?' Dave asks, and Ed starts talking.

He's good, I think, as I listen to him. He's describing the activities that we did, but carefully leaving me out, so that it sounds like he did them on his own. I listen to him talking about the water-skiing, and how he'd done it as a child, then he starts to talk about the windsurfing and the massage. As he moves on to describe the jeep tour, I start to become aware that I need to wee.

They move on to discuss the wedding and how he feels about Sarah now. After a while I stop listening, as the need to wee is getting more and more urgent. I always need to go when I first wake up; I should have got him to hold them off for a few more minutes so I could go to the loo, but everything happened so fast. What am I going to do? I start scanning the room for some sort of suitable receptacle, but there's nothing.

I pick up my watch from the bedside table. How long have they been in there? Maybe, if the hour is nearly done, I can just about hold out. I realise as I look at it that I have no idea what time they started, so I have no way to work out how far through they are. I focus on the conversation again, trying to get a clue. He's talking about how he felt on the wedding day versus how he feels now. It certainly doesn't sound like they're wrapping up.

It's no good. I can't wait any longer. I'm jiggling my legs to try to hold it in, but even that isn't helping. Thankfully, as well as the doors out into the sitting room, there's an interconnecting door from the bedroom into the bathroom, so I can at least get in there undetected. Silently, I slip out of bed, put on a dressing gown and tiptoe into the bathroom. The door from the bathroom into the sitting room is open. I'll have to close it otherwise they'll hear me weeing. Praying that it won't squeak, I start to close it. I turn the handle so it won't click when it engages with the post, and then very gently release it once the door is fully closed. The voices carry on, so I know I'm undetected.

I hurry over to the loo and sit down. I clench my pelvic muscles to try to keep the noise to a minimum, and the relief when I'm done is immense. I wipe myself, stand up and, without thinking about it, press the flusher.

As soon as I've pressed it, I realise my mistake. The cascade of water as the loo flushes feels like the loudest noise I've ever heard, and sure enough, once it subsides, I can tell that the conversation in the other room has stopped. I literally have no idea what to do, so I scamper back into the bedroom and jump into bed, pulling the bedclothes up around me.

'What's going on back there?' Dave's voice sounds suspicious, suddenly. 'What are you hiding from us, Ed?'

I hear footsteps hurrying across the floor and, a couple of seconds later, the bedroom door is flung open and a very unattractive burly man is staring at me with a look of triumph on his face.

'Well now, it looks like Ed's been keeping secrets from us,' he observes, and I recognise him as Dave from his voice. 'Who might you be, darlin'?'

I open my mouth to reply, but before I can say anything, Ed appears.

'What the hell are you doing?' he snarls at Dave. 'Do you make a habit of barging into people's bedrooms? This is private!'

'I don't think so, mate,' Dave sneers as another man, presumably Jamie, appears behind him with a camera, which he instantly focuses on me. 'The production company are paying for all this, aren't they, so we've got "access to all areas". If I want to come in here, I'm completely within my rights. Now, why don't you introduce me to your friend and get out of the way so Jamie can get a decent shot?'

'No.' Ed manoeuvres himself so he's blocking both Dave's path and Jamie's view.

'Look,' Dave begins, using the kind of patient tone that you'd use when trying to pacify a toddler, 'this can play out one of two ways. I can call the production company and tell them you're in breach of your contract, or we can sit down and have a chat with the little lady here.' He sticks his head over Ed's shoulder to address me. 'The viewers are going to love you, darlin'. What a story you'll make!'

'For God's sake, let her get dressed at least!' Ed implores, trying to push them out of the door.

'OK,' Dave concedes. 'We'll wait out here for you. Don't be long!'

As soon as the door is closed, Ed rushes over to me. 'I'm so, so sorry,' he says. He looks absolutely stricken.

'It's my fault,' I tell him. 'I couldn't hold it any longer, and I flushed without thinking.'

'What's done is done. Unfortunately, I don't think there's anything else we can do except face them now. There isn't another way out unless you fancy jumping off the balcony. Will you be OK?'

Of course I'm not going to be OK! I'm going to be on national TV as the consolation prize that Ed picked up on his honeymoon. How the hell am I going to live this down? On the other hand, as Ed says, there's nothing else I can do. I do briefly consider hurling myself off the balcony, but I reluctantly conclude that facing Dave and Jamie is marginally preferable to breaking every bone in my body.

I quickly finish dressing, plaster a smile on my face, take Ed's hand and force myself to walk out into the sitting room with him. I realise I'm clasping my bag to my chest with the other hand, like some sort of security blanket. I don't even remember picking it up.

There are two cameras, both pointing straight at us, with bright lights above them. I'm a literal rabbit in the headlights.

'While we were filming the interview, we became aware that Ed wasn't alone,' Dave says into the microphone. He turns to me and says, 'Why don't you tell us a bit about yourself, and how you got to know Ed.' His voice might be back to professional presenter mode, but he's leering at me in a most unpleasant way. The way he's looking at me makes me feel like a piece of meat. I'm burning with embarrassment and humiliation. I can see the red lights blinking on top of the cameras indicating that they're filming. I can't do this.

'I'm Charlotte,' I manage to say as I drop Ed's hand, 'and, umm, I have to go. Sorry.'

'I don't think so, darlin'.' Dave tries to block my path but I push past him and throw open the door. As soon as I'm outside, I start running as fast as I can. To begin with, I'm aware of Dave panting behind me and calling me back, but it doesn't take me long to outrun him. I don't have a plan for where I'm going, I just know that I need to get away. Away from leering pervy Dave, away from Ed and his honeymoon that I shouldn't have got involved in, away from the shame I'm feeling. As the distance builds between me and the honeymoon suite, I realise I need a plan. I could go back to my room but, if they're going to threaten Ed with breach of contract, he may feel his only option is to come and find me to try to talk me round. I need to get out of the hotel.

I sprint towards reception and, as I approach, I notice a minibus with 'Antigua Boat Tours' painted on the side. A few tourists are already sitting inside. As I run into the reception area, I see the driver talking to one of the receptionists. I dash up and interrupt them.

'Are there any spaces left on the boat tour today?' I ask, breathlessly.

'There are, but we're just leaving now,' the driver replies.

'How much?'

'One hundred and twenty US dollars.'

'OK. Just give me five minutes, please. I'll be as quick as I can.'

He agrees, reluctantly. I hand my credit card to the receptionist to take the money. I give her my room number and, as soon as she's processed the payment, I dash into the hotel shop. I'm still wearing my evening clothes from last night, and I'm going to boil to death if I have to keep those on all day. I find the rack of bikinis and flick through them as fast as I can, looking for one in my size. The only one that I find is skimpy, has a brown and gold swirly pattern on it, and tassels on the bottoms. It's hideous, but there's nothing else. It's also, if I've done the currency conversion right in my head, £70. How can anyone charge that much money for so little material, for goodness' sake? I also find a floppy hat (£30), the cheapest pair of sunglasses I can (£50) and a bottle of sun cream (£15). This is becoming a very expensive escape.

However, beggars can't be choosers. I pay for it all and dash into the changing room to put the bikini on. I stuff my knickers and bra in my bag, don the sunglasses and hat, and I reckon I'm ready to go. As I pass the receptionist, I stop. There's one more thing I need.

'I'm really sorry, but do you have a towel I can borrow for the day?'

'I do,' she replies. 'But you have to pay a deposit.'

Mouthing my apologies at the increasingly impatient driver, I hand over my credit card once again. As soon as it's gone through and the towel is in my hand, he practically pushes me out and onto the bus.

We pull out onto the road and, as the hotel starts to recede from sight, I feel my pulse start to slow. I've pulled it off. I've escaped. The further we get from the hotel, the more relaxed I feel. The bus stops at a few other hotels to pick up customers, and I study each one, looking for clues to indicate whether each hotel is nicer, or not as nice, as ours. It's a welcome distraction from the events of the morning so far.

I realise after a while that I haven't told Mum and Dad where I'm going. They'll assume I'm spending the day with Ed though, as planned, so they won't be worried, unless... Oh no. Ed will be bound to track them down to ask where I am. In my rush to escape I didn't consider them at all. If I call them from my mobile, the cost will be astronomical, but this is an emergency and I'll just have to suck it up and be as brief as I can. I rummage frantically in my bag for my phone, even emptying the other larger items such as my underwater camera onto the seat next to me so I can see more clearly, but it's not there. With a sinking feeling, I realise that it's still attached to its charger on the bedside table in Ed's bedroom, and I'm all alone in a strange country with no way of contacting anyone, let alone Mum and Dad. Oh, God. Can today get any worse? I hurriedly consider my options. I could ask the driver to take me back, I suppose, but given that I've already made him late, I don't think he'll be very receptive to that idea. There's nothing I can do right now. I'll just have to hope for the best and deal with them when I get back.

20

The boat, when we get there, is a catamaran that has definitely seen better days. Music is pumping out from speakers on board, and my heart sinks even further. This looks just like the booze cruise that Ed and I decided to avoid. Kicking myself for my panic back at the hotel, I join the other passengers in the queue to board. Listening to their voices, I realise I'm probably the only English person on the trip, as all the people around me have broad American accents. I allow myself to be swept along and file onto the boat, taking my seat on an empty bench where I hopefully won't be disturbed. I'm proved wrong almost immediately, however.

'Excuse me, honey, are these seats taken?'

I turn to look at the woman addressing me. I guess she's in her early forties, and she is accompanied by a man that I imagine is her husband, plus two surly-looking teenage boys.

'No, please help yourselves,' I reply, as hospitably as I can.

As the boat leaves the jetty and the journey begins, she

introduces herself and her family. I find out that she's called Hannah, her husband is Doug, and their two boys are Joel and Matthew. They're from Connecticut, and they've come to Antigua as part of her fortieth birthday celebrations. She's pleasant to talk to, and chats away to me as the boat heads out to sea. I can't help remarking that she's seems young to be the mother of teenagers.

'Ah well, Doug and I married young,' she tells me. 'We both come from Christian families, and were brought up to believe that sex before marriage was a sin. By the time we were twenty-one, we were pretty much fit to burst, so married as early as we could.' Out of the corner of my eye I can see her boys rolling their eyes with embarrassment, and I flash them a sympathetic smile.

'Don't worry about them,' Hannah assures me. 'They're used to us, aren't you, boys?' The boys studiously ignore her, pretending to be completely absorbed in their phones.

'I've got no regrets,' she continues. 'Doug's a good man, and I love my boys. What about you? Anyone special in your life?'

I don't want to talk about Ed to her, so I tell her I'm currently single. She tells me more about their life in Connecticut, and asks about mine. I try to be polite, but I'm conscious that my answers are verging on the monosyllabic. She doesn't appear to notice though. Given that her children are teenagers, and I don't think Doug has spoken a word since they sat down, she may think that I'm extremely entertaining company in comparison. After a while, the conversation peters out, and I'm left with my thoughts again. Hopefully, pervy Dave and his sidekick Jamie will have given up by the time I get back, and Ed and I can have some time to swap numbers and make a plan before he leaves. It suddenly occurs to me that I have no idea how long this trip actually is.

'Excuse me,' I say to Hannah, 'this is going to sound odd, but I signed up for this very much at the last minute, without really knowing what was involved. Do you have a leaflet or something so I can get an idea of what we're going to do?'

'Sure, honey, no problem!' she says, and hands me a brightly coloured leaflet. It seems we're currently heading out to a reef for some snorkelling, and then we're going to sail on down to an area of mangrove swamps, which we will kayak through with a guide. We'll then have lunch ashore before re-boarding the boat for the return journey up the coast. Bold type informs me that the

BAR WILL BE OPEN!!!

on the return journey. Estimated time of arrival back at the dock is four o'clock in the afternoon.

I do some swift calculations in my head. Allowing time for everyone to get off the boat and back onto the bus, plus the other drop-offs before my hotel, I'm not going to be back before six, by which time Ed will have left for the airport. Three thoughts hit me in quick succession:

Ed's last memory of me will be me running away from him.

I've missed the opportunity to say goodbye to him properly and get his number.

I'm probably never going to see him again.

The last one hits me like a punch in the gut and starts the

tears. I stare resolutely out to the side of the boat as they fall.
The last thing I need is sympathy from a stranger – that will
set me off properly.

* * *

By the time we arrive at the reef, I've recovered a little of my
composure, and I line up behind Hannah and her family to
be issued with snorkels and flippers. We're warned about not
touching the reef itself and given a safety briefing, and then
we're sent off to explore. The water is crystal-clear and I'm
soon floating above the reef, looking down at an amazing
variety of multicoloured fish. I try to capture some of them on
my camera, but they're fast and I suspect I have quite a few
pictures of empty sea. I've seen some of these fish before, on
visits to various aquaria when I was growing up, but I can't
remember the names of any of them. Ed would like this, I
think. My mind flashes back to this morning, to the camera
crew and the way Dave leered at me. Ed was so sweet, the way
he tried to protect me from them. I wonder what would have
happened if we hadn't been interrupted, and we'd had our
last day together as planned. I imagine us arranging to meet
up when we're back home, and an image of us at a cosy pub
somewhere comes to my mind. My stomach does a little
backflip as I entertain the fantasy, but reality crashes in far
too quickly with a much bleaker picture of Ed looking down
from his plane and mentally wishing me goodbye as the
Antiguan coast recedes from view. I don't want to think about
that now. I concentrate on the fish instead and try to
remember the name of at least one of them. A number of

striped fish with yellow streaks swim by, and at last a name comes to me – they're Sergeant Majors, named because the bright stripes look like the insignia of a military sergeant major.

Once back on the boat, I distract myself by asking Hannah, Doug and the boys what they saw. Hannah is convinced that she and Doug saw a parrot fish, but the boys just shrug and bury their noses back in their phones. Hannah turns to me and whispers, conspiratorially, 'They think they're all cool and indifferent, but they're just boys underneath and they're secretly loving it.' I look at them and I'm not convinced.

To be fair to them, the boys do liven up when we get to the mangrove swamp. The kayaks are all designed for two people, so they're busily angling to get one together, rather than one each going with Hannah and Doug, which is Hannah's preference. I seem to be the only person here on my own, so the captain kindly volunteers to come with me. Joel and Matthew set off at top speed, overtaking the guide and whooping as they go, with Hannah and Doug in hot pursuit calling to them to slow down and be careful. The captain, who I learn is also English and called Richard, and I take a more leisurely pace. As we glide through the swamp, he explains about the animals and birds that live there, and why the swamps are so important. When we come out on the other side and circle back to the beach we started from, a barbecue has been set up, and there's a bar serving drinks. We are the last to arrive, and there's already a queue for food.

We pull the kayak onto the beach and join the queue. The food smells great and I realise that I haven't eaten anything today, so I take a little bit of everything. Hannah and her family are on a table that's already full, so I take a seat by myself on another table. Richard comes and joins me.

'I love Americans,' he tells me. 'They're so exuberant when they come on holiday. I think that, because they work so hard and don't get as much holiday time as we do in Europe, they come here determined to make every moment count. Watch them on the boat on the way back when the bar opens. They'll be knocking it back like it's their last day on earth.'

He's not wrong. After lunch, we board the boat and set off on our return journey. Richard announces that we will pop into a couple of interesting bays on the way back, and then tells us that the bar is open. Soon a real party atmosphere has developed on board. I spot Hannah, her face flushed, having an energetic conversation with Doug, who is making steady progress through a beer. He seems to have relaxed and has his arm around her.

I take my towel out onto the deck area at the front of the boat, spread it out and lie down. I need some quiet time to properly digest the events of the last few days and, particularly, this morning. I love Ed, there's no doubt about that, and I've loved every second of our time together. But there's so much I don't know about his real life. For all I know, he might live miles away from me, although I suspect he's probably based within striking distance of London. I have no concrete evidence for this theory beyond an irrational conviction that all hotshot lawyers must be based there. When I look at it more objectively, I realise that he could be based anywhere in the UK. As I realise how little I actually know about him, the sensible part of me tells me to chalk it up as a holiday romance and let him go, but there's another part, deep down, that knows it was much more than that, for both of us. After all, he was the one that wanted to talk about what would happen when we got home, so it was obviously more than a holiday romance for him. I wish we'd had a chance to say goodbye properly, and maybe even make those promises to meet up in the UK that we probably wouldn't keep. Instead, I'm left in a kind of limbo where I'll never know what might have been. Bloody Dave and his stupid, leering face.

Thinking of Dave brings up my second problem. How am I going to cope with being seen as Ed's holiday fling when *Married Before We Met* airs in the autumn? How many people that I know are likely to watch it? Mads will, of course, but I'll tell her the whole story when I get home anyway. Will anyone at work watch it? If Rachel on reception does, then I'm doomed to some serious piss-taking from my colleagues, especially by the time she's added her inevitable enhancements to the story. What about the girls from school? They'll think it's hysterical and we'll have a good laugh together; that'll be fine.

Even though I'm trying hard to blot it out, my mind inevitably makes its way back to this morning. Perhaps I should have had more courage and fronted up to Dave and his camera. I imagine the scenario playing out differently. In this version, I'm calmly answering his questions and coming across as a much more suitable match for Ed than Sarah was. Ed is delighted and has his arm around me as I talk. Back in the real world, I look at my watch. He'll be waiting in reception for his transfer to the airport. I miss him so much already.

When the bus finally drops me back at the hotel, I know that Ed will be long gone, but I call into reception anyway, just in case. I ask if he dropped off my phone, but there's nothing for me when they check, and they promise me the cleaners would have handed it in if they'd found it. My mind is in turmoil as I wander slowly back to my room, trying to work out what could have happened to it. As soon as I put my key in the lock, my parents' door bursts open and they rush out.

'Where have you been? We've been so worried!' my mother cries. 'We were starting to think something had happened to you!'

She wraps her arms around me and I hug her back.

'Are you OK, Charlotte?' Dad asks, sounding equally concerned.

'I'm fine,' I reply. 'I'm sorry you were worried. I needed some time alone and booked an excursion at the last minute. It was only when I was already on the bus that I realised I hadn't told you I was going out, and I'd left my phone behind.'

'We've got that, don't worry,' Dad tells me, and a wave of relief briefly crashes over me, before I realise that means my cover is probably blown.

'How have you got it?' I ask, nervously. 'I'm pretty sure I know where I left it.'

'Ed gave it to us. When you didn't appear at breakfast this morning, we assumed you were with him and didn't think anything about it, but when he came to find us, told us you'd left your phone behind in his room and asked if we knew where you were, we started to worry. Your father searched the entire resort. He even called into reception to ask if they'd seen you, but of course they wouldn't tell him anything because of client confidentiality,' my mother tells me.

'I really am sorry,' I say.

'What happened? Was it Ed? You two made such a lovely couple, and he was obviously worried. Did you have a row?'

'What makes you think we were a couple?'

'For goodness' sake, Charlotte!' she exclaims. 'We didn't come down in the last shower, you know. You kept saying you were tired and going to bed early, but when we came back from the bar your room was in darkness and the curtains were still open, so you obviously weren't in it. We heard you when you came back in the mornings. We were pleased that you'd found someone, especially someone as lovely as Ed.'

Of course she knows. Why do I ever bother trying to hide anything from her? She's like a Rottweiler. I give her the basics, explaining about Dave, and me dashing out, and just needing to be far away. She's sympathetic, but Dad finds the whole thing uproariously funny for some reason.

'Oh, Charlotte,' he breathes through his laughter, 'all that fuss over some saddo with a camera and a TV programme that only you and Madison watch. What on earth are we going to do with you?'

I'm tempted to tell him that the true viewing figures are actually in the millions, but I decide to take pity on him. There's nothing he can do about it, and he'll only worry.

'Ed also left a note, by the way,' Dad says. 'I'll just get it.'

He disappears into their room, returning a couple of seconds later with my phone, the charger and a piece of paper. I open it and read:

Dear Charley,

I'm SO sorry about this morning. Don't worry about the TV programme – I've sorted it.

*If you want to call me when you get back to the UK, my
number is below. I'd love to hear from you.*

Love

Ed xx

What does he mean, he's sorted it?

Never mind that, I realise. He's given me his number.

21

I was very tempted to call Ed as soon as I'd plugged his number into my phone last night, but he obviously wouldn't have answered on the plane, and I'll want to talk to him for hours, so I've decided to wait until I get back. I also toyed with sending him a WhatsApp, but I have no idea whether he uses it. In the end, I decided to keep it as something to look forward to when I get home. He wants to hear from me again, and that's enough to buoy me up for now.

After breakfast, I wander down to the beach and head for my usual sunlounger on autopilot. As I get close, I see that it's already occupied, as is the one next to it. A young couple, obviously very much in love, are lying down and staring into each other's eyes. They must be the new occupants of the honeymoon suite. I beat a retreat to another sunlounger and pull out my book. I'm finding it difficult to concentrate though, and after a while I walk down to the water sports hut to enquire about some more windsurfing and water-skiing lessons. I've got another week of holiday to go, so I reason I might as well make the most of it. I learn that the windsurfing is included in the all-inclusive package, but the water-skiing is not, so I hand over my credit card and book a windsurfing lesson for each morning, and water-skiing every afternoon.

Over the remainder of the holiday, a routine develops. I wake, have a shower, put a bikini on under shorts and a T-shirt and then meet my parents for breakfast. After breakfast, I lie on the beach and read until it's time for my windsurfing lesson. I meet up with Mum and Dad for lunch, and then head back to the beach for water-skiing. After that I read until it's time to get changed and go to the bar before dinner. I'm doing my best to enjoy the remainder of the holiday, but I'm aware that I'm also counting down the days until we go home and I can call Ed.

My muscles complain for the first couple of days but, as I grow in confidence and my body gets used to the exertion, the aches subside and I can feel myself making progress. By the third day, I'm able to sail the windsurfer pretty confidently and I'm heading further out into the bay. I'm also feeling much more secure on the water-skis, and don't fall over at all. The instructors start showing me how to weave from side to side behind the boat, and also how to ski with just one hand on the handle.

For our final evening, Mum and Dad have booked us into the Asian restaurant again. Although I'm now really excited about going home and getting back in touch with Ed, I don't want to take my last twenty-four hours here for granted. I have no idea when I'm ever going to get to experience another holiday like this, so I'm determined to make the most of my final day here. Mum and Dad are on great form, and we make steady progress through the bottle of white wine Dad has ordered to go with our dinner. By the time the starters have been cleared, the bottle is already empty and I notice the waiter discreetly lift it out of the ice bucket that's sunk into the middle of the table and replace it with another one. I watch my parents as they talk and it's clear to me that, even after all these years, they completely adore each other. I grab my phone out of my bag and take a picture to capture the moment; maybe Ed and I will be like that one day.

Over the main course, Mum gently grills me about where I think my relationship with Ed is going, but I'm thankfully just sober enough to head her off. Dad is still guffawing about the whole incident with the film crew. I'm starting to suspect it's been the high point of his holiday.

'Right, Christine,' he announces when the waiter brings the dessert menu, 'it's the last night, and you know what that means.'

'He's going to order the celebration sundae,' Mum tells me when I look at her quizzically. 'It's not Asian at all, but it is the most ridiculous thing and he seems to think it's some sort of ritual to end the holiday with.'

Sure enough, when the desserts come out, Dad is presented with a bowl so large that a family of goldfish could happily live in it. It's filled with various ice creams, sorbets, tropical fruit pieces and, just to make sure your arteries stand no chance, what appears to be the entire contents of a can of squirty cream. There are also the obligatory wafers, but what really draws the eye are the sparklers. It's the most over-the-top thing I've ever seen and I reach for my phone to capture it before the sparklers burn out.

'Have you seen my phone?' I ask Mum, as soon as I realise it isn't on the table where I put it after the last photo.

'Didn't you put it back in your bag?'

'I don't think so.' I'm fairly certain it was on the table, but I make a brief check of my bag anyway and, as I expected, it isn't there. I push back my chair and start peering under the table. The atmospheric lighting doesn't help, but I'm still able to tell it hasn't fallen on the floor. I stand up to see if I can get a better view, and my heart sinks when I spot a familiar-looking dark shadow under the bottle of wine in the ice bucket.

'Fuck!' I exclaim as I hastily reach into the bucket and pull out the sodden phone. I press the home button but, unsurprisingly, nothing happens.

'Shit, shit, shit!' I press the button repeatedly, hoping that my phone will magically burst back into life, but the screen stays dark.

'How did it get in there?' Mum asks.

'Maybe the waiter knocked it when he was clearing the plates, or maybe I hit it accidentally, I don't know!'

'Don't panic. You just need some rice,' Dad reassures me. He flags down a waiter and, before long, my phone is encased in a plastic container full of basmati rice.

'The rice draws the moisture out of the phone,' he tells me. 'Leave it in there overnight and try it in the morning.'

'What if it still isn't working?'

'Is it insured?'

I think back to the reams of paperwork I filled in when I

was in the mobile phone store with Mads. I'm certain there was one about accidental damage insurance.

'I think so.'

'Then there's nothing to worry about, is there?'

The next morning, the phone is still completely dead, but I'm certain that I did take out the insurance so, although I won't be able to call Ed the moment the plane lands like I planned to, it should be a fairly straightforward process to get it replaced when I take it in. If I'm lucky, they'll be able to read the memory card, or whatever it is, and retrieve the pictures of Mum and Dad as well. I'm feeling relaxed as I head out on the windsurf board towards the beach that Ed and I kayaked to. I spend some time tacking back and forth, enjoying the feeling of being in control and harnessing the wind to go where I want to go. I've splashed out at the hotel shop and bought myself a little GoPro camera that I strap to the board, so I can record myself and watch it back once I'm home. I head around the far side of the bay before turning back towards the beach. The sun is high in the sky and I can sense its warmth on my skin. As I come back into the shallows, being careful to avoid the area where the swimmers are, I spot two familiar figures watching me.

I hand the board and life jacket back and wander out to where Mum and Dad are standing.

'Blimey, Charlotte!' my dad exclaims. 'You looked like a pro!'

I hug him. 'Thanks, Dad. How long were you watching for?'

'A good half-hour I'd say. You were miles out across the bay, and we had to ask the instructors which one was you. We thought we might come and watch some of your water-skiing this afternoon if that's OK?'

'Of course!'

The afternoon ski session also goes well. We fix the GoPro to the back of the boat before we set off, and I rise smoothly out of the water as we head out across the bay. I practise weaving in and out of the boat's wake, as well as some one-handed holds. Of the two water sports I've mastered, this is definitely my favourite. The breeze, the spray, the speed and the constant movement of the skis beneath me as I cross the wake of the boat makes me feel truly alive. I'm in awe of the strength of my body, controlling my balance and keeping me upright as we power around the bay. At the end of the session we come back in towards the beach and, as I sink back into the water, I can see my parents applauding.

Mum and Dad have arranged for a late checkout, so I'm able to head back to my room to shower and get changed before we leave for the airport.

As the plane takes off that evening, I settle back into my seat with a glass of champagne and think about what I'm going back to. The first priority will be sorting out my phone and getting in touch with Ed, but I'm also looking forward to moving into my flat and getting on with the next part of my life, whatever that looks like. I realise that, apart from a couple of conversations when I first met Ed, I've hardly thought about Josh at all. After dinner, I put my seat down into its flat position, cover myself with the blanket, and drift off to sleep.

Waking in business class is a weird experience. The air of quiet sophistication from the evening before is gone; there are pillows and rumpled blankets everywhere and everyone looks dishevelled and bleary-eyed, apart from the cabin crew, who are coming round with breakfast. I join the queue for the loo to try to sort out the worst of the damage, eat my breakfast and drink two cups of coffee to try to wake myself up properly. Shortly after the stewardess has cleared my table, the captain announces that we're beginning our descent into London.

England is much as we left it: cold, grey and miserable. After two weeks in the warm sunshine, my body is unprepared for the chill that strikes us as we get off the plane and start the long trudge towards immigration and the baggage reclaim. There's no business class privilege here; immigration is heaving with people arriving from all around the world, and the queues are long. Dour-faced officials direct tired travellers towards the e-gates or manned desks, depending on their passport. Every so often someone gets stuck in an e-gate, and they're hustled away to join the even bigger queue for manned immigration. There's none of the anticipation and excitement of the departure lounge here, only weariness and an over-whelming desire to be anywhere else.

Once we've finally cleared immigration, there's another long wait to see which baggage carousel the luggage from our flight will be unloaded onto. All the overnight flights seem to have landed at once and there are people milling about every-where. Every so often a flight flashes up on the board with a carousel number and a load of people rush off to secure the best spots to get their luggage as quickly as they can. When our turn comes, Dad manoeuvres himself into a decent posi-tion but, despite the priority tags, our bags don't seem to arrive any faster than anyone else's. Eventually, we make our way through customs and out to the taxi.

The house is warm and inviting when we get back. The house-sitter heads off, and I take my bags upstairs. I stand under the shower, letting it wash the grime of the flight away, and then set about the task of unpacking. Most of my clothes are dirty and I'll have to wash them, so I lob them into my dirty clothes basket to deal with later. I need to get to Blue-water and sort out my phone so I can call Ed.

22

'What do you mean, you can't retrieve any data?' I ask the man in the mobile phone shop.

'It's the way these phones work,' he explains. 'All the data, your pictures, contacts and so on, are stored in the phone's internal memory. We can only get to that by powering it up and, since we can't power it up, we can't retrieve the data. Did you turn on the online backup feature?'

'The what?'

'In the menu system, there's an online backup option. Did you turn that on?'

'I didn't even know it existed.'

'OK, we'll take that as a "no", then. We can replace your phone under the insurance you took out, that's not a problem. The SIM card also appears undamaged, so there's no issue there. But if you didn't have the online backup turned on, then I'm afraid you'll have to enter all your contacts again. What I will do, however, is show you how to turn it on so this doesn't happen again.'

'But what am I going to do about my contacts? I don't know anyone's phone number off by heart!' I exclaim. That isn't strictly true. I know Josh's phone number, but that's not exactly one I want to keep.

'Are you on social media?' the man asks.

'Yes.'

'Then put out a post explaining that your phone got damaged, and ask everyone to text you their number. That's what most people do.'

It's not his fault, I remind myself, and what he's saying does make sense. But I can't get my head around the fact that the one number I needed above all else, the number I was looking forward to calling so much, is trapped forever in the waterlogged memory of my iPhone, and Ed's note is probably still in the drawer of my bedside table in Antigua where I put it for safekeeping. I'm so frustrated, I'm struggling not to cry.

The man is very helpful and helps me set up the online backup system, but if ever there was a case of shutting the stable door long after the horse has bolted, this has to be it.

I'm still in the doldrums when Mads calls to welcome me home later that afternoon. It sounds like she's outdoors in a force nine gale.

'Where are you?' I ask her.

'Scotland, researching an article about shooting holidays. Honestly, Charley, I don't think I've ever seen so much mud. I can't wait to get back home on Friday. How was the holiday?'

I fill her in on the details. She's very excited to hear about Ed, as I knew she would be.

'Did you get back on the horse?' she asks.

'There might have been a certain amount of riding, yes,' I reply, coyly.

She shrieks down the phone. 'Good for you!! Nothing like a new shag to blast away the cobwebs of the old. So, are you seeing him again?'

I tell her about the phone, and she sighs. 'That's too bad. But if he's half the hotshot lawyer he says he is, he shouldn't be hard to find, should he? Have a look on the internet, I bet you'll find him. Are you all set to move on Saturday?'

'Yes, looking forward to it. Are you still coming to help, or do you think you'll be too tired after your Scottish exploits?'

'I'll be there, don't worry. Now, go and track down your man and we'll make a plan when I'm back.'

She rings off and I realise she's right. It shouldn't be that hard to track him down on the internet. I don't know the name of his company, so I start with Facebook. There are literally thousands of people called Ed Wells on there, and I start trawling through them one by one. After a while, I feel my eyelids starting to droop, so I make a note of where I've got to and go downstairs to collect my latest load of laundry. It's only a couple of days until I move, so I need to get everything organised.

The jet lag is obviously muddling my head, because it takes me until the next day to think to check LinkedIn, where I find him fairly quickly and send a message explaining about the accident with my phone and leaving him my number. I don't know how often he checks it and he could be up to his neck in a complex case for all I know, so I try to be patient, but it's starting to get difficult by the time Saturday comes around and there is still no reply. Mads arrives early and together we load my stuff into the Fiesta. When we're done, I double-check the room to make sure I haven't missed anything. I go into the kitchen to say goodbye to Mum, only to find she's a bit tearful.

'I'm only moving to Tonbridge, Mum!' I tell her. 'It's hardly the other side of the world, and I'll drop in often.'

'I know—' she sniffs '—but I've got used to having you around and the house is going to feel empty without you.'

'You'll be fine,' I tell her. 'Apart from anything else, you've got Simon, Emma, the girls and the puppy coming tomorrow. What have they called it again?'

'Lulu,' she reminds me.

'Exactly, so you've got meeting Lulu for the first time to look forward to. Focus on that.'

Dave, the agent, meets us at the flat. There are a couple of forms to fill in and then he hands me the keys. He shows me how to work the remote control to get in and out of the secure parking area, and then leaves us to it. A couple of hours later, everything is in and I've unpacked. Mads is fiddling with the complicated-looking coffee machine to see if she can get a flat white out of it. I slump on the sofa, taking in my new surroundings.

'I give up,' she announces after a few more minutes. 'Let's make a list of stuff that you need to buy and go and get a coffee from that shop you were telling me about.'

'Well, apart from bedding, I guess I need a cafetière, so I don't have to fight with that thing in the mornings, and some food. Do you want to stay for dinner?'

We make a list of what we need and head out on the first trip. Next to Sainsbury's there's a department store where I find all the bedding I need, as well as the cafetière. We take it back to the flat and make the bed, and then head out again to the coffee shop to reward ourselves. I find us a table and Mads goes to investigate the cakes.

When she returns with two flat whites and two slices of carrot cake, I fill her in on the silence from Ed.

'Show me his profile,' she instructs.

I load up the LinkedIn page, slightly embarrassed to note that I've obviously been there often enough that my phone now prompts me with the full address, and hand her the phone.

She takes it from me and studies him while she chews a piece of carrot cake.

'Interesting,' she says at last. 'Not what I would have pictured as your type, but he's got a nice face. He's certainly a step up from Josh. How was the sex?'

'Really? You're going to do this now?'

'Why, wasn't it any good?'

'It was very nice, if you must know.'

'Hmm. I'm guessing it was better than very nice, because you're being surprisingly coy about it.' She smiles.

'It's not just about the sex,' I caution her.

'Oh, I know. I'm sure you had lots of romantic strolls and gazed into each other's eyes under the stars, and all that stuff. But if the sex is no good, none of that really counts.'

I don't know how to reply to that, so I sit back as she scrolls around the site a bit more and sips her coffee.

'Right,' she pronounces, after a few minutes. 'It was a good idea, but looking at his profile it looks to me as if he set up the account and hasn't used it since. There's no activity that I can see at all. Normally, you'd expect to see some job updates, maybe some qualifications, and a network of connections. This has none of those. So, I don't think he's seen your message. But you know where he works now, so maybe you can get in touch that way. Shall we go and get something for tonight?'

We head into the supermarket, where I stock up on the essentials before she helps me to take it all back to the flat and unpack it. Having done that, she settles herself into the sofa and watches as I start to prepare something for us to eat. After a while she speaks again.

'It's nice here. I like it. I think you'll be very happy.'

'I hope so,' I reply. It's true. The flat has a good feel to it, and I'm looking forward to curling up in my new bedding later. I'm a little intimidated by some of the appliances; as well as the coffee machine that Mads couldn't fathom out, the dish-washer and washer-dryer both look much more complicated than they need to be. Thankfully, the owner has left instruction manuals, so I'll check those out when I need to.

Over dinner, Mads fills me in on her Scottish trip and shows me pictures of a couple of guys she's currently messaging on Tinder. They're fairly standard Mads fare and I'm sure she'll chew them up and spit them out in the same way that she does with most men. After we've eaten, we wash up, and Mads heads off.

I wake late the next morning, fix myself a coffee and take it back to bed, along with my laptop. I fire it up, open the browser and navigate to LinkedIn. Unlike my phone, this hasn't remembered the full address of Ed's profile page, so it takes a little longer to find him. When I do, I spend a while just gazing at him before getting on with the next step. I enter

Watson & Fletcher into the search box and click the link for the company.

It's a very slick, professional website. I learn that, as well as divorce, they handle pre- and post-nuptial agreements and a variety of family law issues, such as relocation of children when one partner wishes to move abroad. It all sounds fairly depressing to me. I don't know how I'd feel about signing a prenup. I think I'd feel pissed off that I wasn't completely trusted. But then, if the shoe was on the other foot and I was some kind of millionaire, would I want to protect myself from a husband potentially grabbing half of it after shagging his secretary? If you love and trust someone enough to marry them, surely you have to take some risks, don't you? I guess the kind of people that Ed's firm looks after have more than just the odd million though, so maybe they all think it's completely normal.

I click around the site, looking to see if there are any pictures of Ed, or even an email address. After twenty minutes, I admit defeat. The only pictures are of the two founders. John Watson is a big guy, with dark hair that I'm sure comes out of a bottle, and Mark Fletcher is thin and wiry, with short grey hair. I would imagine they're both in their sixties. The contact page just lists the office address, phone number and a generic email. I note down the phone number. I'll call in the week.

After I've got dressed, I load the footage from the GoPro onto my laptop and watch it. It's come out really well. It takes me a while to fathom out the movie-maker software but, after a few hours, I manage to stitch together some footage of me windsurfing and water-skiing, add some music underneath, and upload it to Facebook. Within moments I've got likes from some of my school friends. Paula comments, 'Wow, look at you!' and Sam writes, 'If I wasn't in love with Louise, I'd be in love with you!' to which I reply, 'Sorry, babe, but you're not my type!'

After lunch, I put the card from the waterproof camera into the laptop and browse through the pictures to decide which ones to print. There are a few of the hotel, which I delete, a couple of Mum, Dad and me on our first night, which they'll like, and then loads of Ed. There's Ed water-skiing – definitely going to print one of those – Ed on a sunlounger, Ed with his kayak, and a few of him and the dinner he laid on for me. There are the pictures from our jeep tour, a couple of nice ones of Ed trying different fruit and a selfie of the two of us at Shirley Heights. I highlight a few of those for printing too. Finally, there are the pictures from the boat tour. As I suspected I did get quite a few pictures of empty sea, but there are a couple with some blurry fish in them, and one that I'm quite pleased with.

Once I've decided which photos to print and deleted the others off the card, I head out to Boots. A while later I return with the prints and a selection of frames. I spend the remainder of the afternoon happily framing them and putting them around the flat.

* * *

The difficulty of having Ed's work number is that I can only really call during office hours, when I'm also busy, so I don't get the opportunity to call him until Wednesday afternoon. I feel nervous as I dial.

'Watson and Fletcher. How may I direct your call?' The voice is female with a slight Eastern European accent.

'Can I speak with Ed Wells, please?' I ask.

'Putting you through.'

My heart is thumping. I'm about to speak to him. Will he be pleased to hear from me?

'Good afternoon, Ed Wells' office. How may I help you?' It's not Ed, the voice is female. The receptionist must have put me through to the wrong extension.

'I'm sorry. I was hoping to speak to Ed Wells,' I tell her.

'Mr Wells is busy at the moment.' I notice her emphasise the 'Mr' as if to scold me for my familiarity. I decide that, whoever she is, I don't like her.

'I'm Alice, his PA,' she continues. 'Is there something I can help you with?' Of course, I'd completely forgotten about the PA.

'I wonder if you would mind taking a message,' I say. 'My name is Charley, and I'm a friend of his. We met on holiday in Antigua, and he gave me his phone number, but I had an accident with my phone and—'

She cuts me off, and I can tell by the tone of her voice that she's taken against me as much as I have her. 'I'm sorry to interrupt you, but would I be right in thinking that you would like to leave a number for Mr Wells to contact you on?'

Snotty cow. Yes, I might have been rambling a little, but there's no need to be rude. Swallowing the words that I'd like to say to her, I put on my most grateful tone instead.

'Thank you, yes please.'

'Remind me of your name?'

'Charlotte, Charlotte Jenkins, although he knows me as Charley—'

'Charley it is,' she interrupts again. 'And the number?'

I reel it off, she reads it back and assures me she'll pass it on, before the line goes dead.

I spend the rest of the afternoon trying to get on with mundane tasks like laundry and cleaning the flat, but the reality is that I'm completely focused on my phone. I check it repeatedly to make sure it's not on silent and that it has plenty of charge. I even check for missed calls every so often, even though it's never out of my sight for a moment. Nothing comes. Even though I'm growing increasingly impatient and frustrated, I'm also trying to be rational. He's probably got back-to-back meetings, maybe an evening engagement. He'll be waiting until he's got a good hour free so we can catch up properly.

After a week of checking my phone every morning, every lunch break and being glued to it every evening, it's starting to dawn on me that he's not going to call. When it finally does ring, I jump out of my skin and nearly drop it in my excitement, but it turns out to be Mads, not Ed.

'He hasn't called!' I wail. 'I don't understand it. Why give me his number and then ghost me?'

'Hmm,' she replies, after I've filled her in on all the details. 'I'd want to hear it from the horse's mouth if it were me. Try and bypass the PA if you can.'

'How am I going to do that?'

'You could try calling at lunchtime – maybe she goes out then? You said he often works late in the evenings, so you could try after hours. Or you could go old school and write him a letter – you have the company address after all.'

I follow her advice and try at about seven that evening, but of course there's nobody manning the switchboard so I just get a generic message telling me the company office hours. I also try at lunchtime, and she's obviously not there because she doesn't answer, but neither does he and the call goes to her voicemail. There seems no point in leaving a message that she will only delete, so in the end I take Mads' advice and write to him.

> *Dear Ed,*
>
> *I'm so sorry that I ran off. I was spooked by the cameras and I didn't know what else to do. Thanks for leaving your phone number, but would you believe I broke my phone? I'd love to hear from you and maybe meet up for a coffee if you have time. My phone number is below.*
>
> *Love*
>
> *Charley xx*

I add my number, address it to him care of his company and take it to work with me. In return for a contribution to the staff biscuit fund Rachel franks it for me and agrees to send it out with the rest of the practice mail.

* * *

Another week passes and I hear nothing. He must have got the letter by now. I've harangued Rachel several times and she's assured me each time that she definitely franked it and she definitely posted it. Despite her penchant for gossip, she is efficient so I do believe her, but why hasn't Ed got in touch?

In the end, I can bear it no more and I decide to run the gauntlet of the PA again. My hands are actually shaking as I dial the number and ask to be put through. I'm greeted by the same PA; I would recognise that voice anywhere.

'I'm really sorry to bother you,' I tell her, with my heart in my mouth. 'My name is Charlotte Jenkins, and I rang a couple of weeks ago and left a message for Ed, I mean, Mr Wells? I haven't heard back from him and I just wanted to check whether you'd managed to pass on the message?'

'I did pass it on,' she tells me, and her voice is pure ice. 'Mr Wells has asked me not to put you through. I'd appreciate if you would stop calling now. Goodbye.'

The line goes dead. The bitch has hung up on me!

23

Months have gone by, and Mads and I have forensically picked over every possible reason for Ed blocking me. Some of them were more plausible than others, and some were downright ludicrous, such as him mistaking me for someone else. How many Charleys did he meet in Antigua, for goodness' sake? In the end, I reluctantly came to the conclusion that he obviously saw me as nothing more than a holiday romance in the end, despite his protestations to the contrary. He probably got home, had a bit of a roasting from his friends and family for signing up to *Married Before We Met* in the first place, and decided to lick his wounds and pick up his old life as if none of it, including me, had ever happened. Mads is less forgiving, but I just can't bring myself to believe that he would give me his number and then block me without a good reason. I don't tell her, but there's a tiny part of me hanging on to an even tinier hope that he might still get in touch, even if it's just to explain.

I'm scrolling through Facebook on my lunch break one day

when I spot a notification. Someone has sent me a friend request. I feel a brief, idiotic surge of hope that this might be him, and eagerly press to see who it is.

It's not Ed.

It's Josh.

My initial disappointment turns to confusion. Josh doesn't believe in social media, and Facebook in particular. 'It's corrosive,' he used to say. 'People think they're more in touch with each other because of it, but actually they're lonelier and more isolated than ever because it's not a real connection. If you want to connect with someone, you should ring them up or go to see them.' So why is he using it now, and why, after months of total silence, does he think it's OK just to send me a friend request as if nothing had ever happened? I'm annoyed and curious in equal measure. In the end, curiosity wins out and I accept it. I can always un-friend him later, after all.

I scroll through his feed to see what I can learn. There's hardly anything personal there; it seems like he's just using it as a platform to promote Earthkind. Most of his posts feature Earthkind products, with links to the site. I look at his friends list. There are a few names I recognise and, of course, Scarlett's is one of them. I switch over to his personal details. He's entered the bare minimum, so there's not much to be learned there and the relationship information is blank. I head back into my treatment room for the afternoon session none the wiser.

When I get home that evening, I notice that there's a message on the app. I open it up and it's Josh again.

'Hi,' is all it says.

I decide to call Mads before I reply. 'Josh sent me a friend request on Facebook at lunchtime,' I tell her, 'and now he's messaging me. Don't you think that's odd?'

'What does he want?'

'I have no idea. I don't know whether to reply or not. What do you think I should do?'

She considers for a few moments. 'Interesting. Now that I come to think about it, I haven't seen Scarlett for a while. Maybe they've split up and he wants you back. How would you feel about that?'

'Josh and I are ancient history now,' I tell her. 'I've moved on, and I have no interest in going back.'

'Plus you're still mooning over Ed,' she replies.

'I'm not!' I retort. 'I don't think he's the bastard you do, but I'm not "mooning" over him.'

'Of course you aren't. That's why your whole flat is practically a shrine to him.'

'Bloody hell, Mads, you're impossible sometimes! Yes, I have a few pictures with him in them, but—'

'Twelve,' she interrupts. 'I counted them. Twelve pictures in a flat made up of three rooms, one of which is the bathroom, so it doesn't count. That's a shrine, trust me. Anyway, we're getting off topic here. How do you feel about Josh's message?'

'I don't know. I am a bit curious to see what he wants, but I'm not sure I want him barging back into my life. I guess it won't do any harm to reply, will it?'

'I have no idea, but you're not going to find out any more unless you do, are you?'

'You're right,' I tell her. 'I'll reply and see what he wants. Oh, and it's not a bloody shrine!'

'It so is!' She laughs and rings off.

I go back to the message. 'Hi,' I type, and hit 'send'.

Immediately, I can see that he's typing, and I realise I should have checked he wasn't online before answering him. I'm not sure I want to do this in real time. I'd envisaged having time to consider my replies between each message. This is too immediate.

His reply comes in:

I wasn't sure you'd accept my friend request.

I send back:

I wasn't sure I would either.

He starts typing again. It's obviously a long one so I put the phone down and go to pour myself a glass of wine. If I'm going to have to talk to Josh, I might as well have a drink. I look around the room. The owner's abstract art is still on the walls, but the pictures I printed and framed are dotted about on some of the surfaces. It's fair to say that they mostly have Ed in them, but I think Mads is a little unfair to describe it as a shrine.

My phone pings, and I wander back to the sofa to see what Josh has said.

I treated you really badly and I just want you to know how sorry I am for that. After all our time together, you deserved better and I quite understand if you hate me. If it's any consolation Mum and Dad were furious too. We didn't speak for a few months.

I'm surprised by how pleased I am about his parents' reaction. I expect they would have really put him through the mill. However, that doesn't alter the fact that this apology is seven months too late. I type:

Why have you decided to say this now?

If he thinks I'm some sort of Labrador that's just going to roll over and ask for my tummy to be rubbed because he's being nice to me, then he's going to be disappointed. I press 'send' and wait for his reply. It's another long one.

A lot of stuff has changed for me since Christmas. I don't want to sound like a hippy, but it's been a journey of discovery. As part of that I realised two things. One, that I needed to apologise properly to you, and two, that I have you to thank for a lot of where I am today.

I type:

I'm glad for you.

I'm still not accepting this apology yet.

Does Scarlett know you're messaging me?

We split up a couple of months ago.

Interesting. Maybe he does want me back. Hastily, I type:

I'm sorry to hear that. I hope you don't think apologising to me
now is going to change anything between us. I've moved on.

There's a brief pause before he replies:

No hidden agenda. Promise. I just wanted the opportunity to apologise in person and say thank you. Would you allow me to buy you
a drink sometime?

He wants to meet? I'm not sure I'm up for that. Even the
conversation we're having now feels a bit intrusive – I don't
think I want to see him face to face. I take my wine out onto
the balcony and look down at the river. A family of ducks are
swimming past, and I watch them while I try to work out what
to do. I hear my phone ping in the sitting room, but I ignore it.

I try to play out meeting up with Josh in my head. It feels
wrong and awkward. I've had all this time to get over him, how
dare he come waltzing back in now? I've rebuilt my life and,
despite the Ed setback, I'm reasonably happy. This feels like
he's trying to drive a bulldozer right through the middle of it. I
stalk back inside and grab my phone.

The message reads:

Are you still there?

I reply to him:

Yes, and I don't think that is a very good idea.

I mute the phone and turn on the TV. I've had enough of

Josh for today. However, just before I go to bed, curiosity gets the better of me and I have a quick check to see if he's replied. There's one message, and it reads:

I understand. If you change your mind, I'll be in the Jolly Farmer between 7 and 9 on Friday.

* * *

'I think you should go,' Mads says, when I ring her up the next day to tell her about it.

'Why on earth do you think that?'

'You're thinking about this from the wrong angle. Last time he saw you, you were, and I say this lovingly, a bit drab. Don't you want to show him what he's missing out on? How fabulous you are now?'

I laugh. 'Don't spare my feelings, will you!'

'I'm only telling you what you know is true. What kind of friend would I be if I wasn't honest with you?'

'Well, I always know where I stand with you. I'll give you that!'

'Exactly. So, my view, which you're welcome to ignore, is that you should go and show him how amazing you are now he's not there to hold you back. Think about it at least?'

I agree and we hang up.

Over the next few days, I consider what she's said. On the one hand, I'm still not wild about the idea of meeting up with Josh. I worry that he'll assume I've forgiven him. A few scribbled lines of apology on Messenger and suddenly it's all forgotten? I don't think so. On the other hand, it would be quite satisfying to see his face when he clocks the new me for the first time. I think about what I could wear, and a few options come to mind.

The other reason I'm tempted to accept his invitation is Scarlett. I can't deny that I'm curious to find out why they split up. Who dumped who and why? Wouldn't it be the cruellest irony if she'd cheated on him? I can't help smiling at the prospect, and my mind is made up.

24

The pub is busy when I get there, and I can't see Josh straight away. I walk through the bar, scanning the tables as I go, and eventually spot him near the back. He doesn't see me, and that gives me a couple of moments to study him surreptitiously.

He's grown a beard. It's neatly trimmed and actually quite suits him. It makes him look more mature somehow. His hair is cut shorter too, and the floppy fringe has gone. He's wearing a well-ironed white T-shirt, and there's what appears to be a black leather jacket on the seat next to him.

'Hello, Josh,' I say as I sit down. His eyes widen in surprise.

'Bloody hell, Charley! You look amazing! I don't think I would have recognised you. You've had your hair cut. It really suits you.'

I have to confess that I did take quite a bit of time getting ready for this. I've gone for the maximum 'see what you're missing' look, with a plunge bra, close-fitting low-cut top, and a pair of white skinny jeans. I smile at him.

'Thank you,' I say. 'Nice beard, and is that a leather jacket?'

'Vegan leather,' he tells me. 'It's made from sustainable materials. Sorry, let me get you a drink – what would you like?'

I ask for a Diet Coke as I'm driving, and he goes off to the bar. I watch him as he gets the server's attention and places his order. He definitely seems more grown up and self-assured. I grudgingly admit that Scarlett seems to have done him some good.

'So,' I say to him after he's come back, placed the drinks on the table and sat down.

'I'm so pleased you came,' he tells me. 'I wasn't sure you would.'

'Neither was I. However, I'm here now. What do you need to tell me?' I've role-played this conversation in a few different ways over the last day or so, and I've decided to go with cool and aloof, to make him squirm.

'Firstly, I'm sorry. I mean it, Charley. I could offer you various excuses, but the plain truth is that I behaved like a shit, and you deserve much better.'

'You did, and I do. Look, Josh, I'm not going to tell you that it's fine, that I'm over it now and it's all water under the bridge. I am over you, but that doesn't alter the fact that you cheated on me. It's bad enough that you were having sex with Scarlett behind my back, but to have sex with her in our bed? That's more than shitty, in my book.'

He looks suitably chastised, and it makes me feel good. I feel in control of this conversation, and powerful.

'I know,' he replies. 'Believe me, I'd do anything to go back and do things differently, but I can't. All I can do is tell you how sorry I am.'

'Why now? Is this because you and Scarlett have split up?

Are you hoping I'll say it's all OK and come running back to you?'

'No, of course not! Scarlett and I split up in April, so I can assure you it's not some weird rebound thing. I've known since it happened that I needed to apologise, but you were so angry, and then time sort of passed, and it became harder and harder to do.'

'Of course I was angry!' I can feel my voice rising and I hastily bring it back under control. 'You basically took ten years of my life and flushed them down the toilet. I'd say that's good grounds to be royally pissed off, wouldn't you?'

'Yes, of course it is, and all I can do is repeat how sorry I am. I've missed you, Charley. You've been such a big part of my life and, although I know we can never have what we had before, I hoped we might be able to be friends at least.'

The fight starts to go out of me. He's so penitent that it's not fun any more; it's starting to feel cruel, like kicking a wounded animal. 'I don't know, Josh. My life is pretty sorted right now, and I'm not sure if I want you back in it in any capacity. I came tonight because I wanted to hear what you had to say, but I'm not going to make any promises after this evening, OK?'

He nods.

'So, what happened with Scarlett?' I ask him.

He sighs. 'It was like living in a tornado, and never knowing which way it was going to go next. She'd have these sudden rages that would go on for days, and just when I was getting to the point where I couldn't take any more and was contemplating ending it, she'd suddenly be sweetness and light again. It was exhausting. I spent my time walking on eggshells around her, terrified that something I'd say or do would set her off. And the mess! I swear that woman could manage to use every pot and pan just to make a salad. In the end I think we both knew it wasn't working and we agreed to end it. I was so relieved when she moved out.'

'But don't you have to work with her? Isn't that awkward?'

'No, that's the second part of what I wanted to say to you tonight. I've moved departments. In fact, I'm now the head buyer for Earthkind, and it's all thanks to you!'

'Me? How?'

'Your rant about the Earthkind range got me thinking. You were right that, although they had the environmental credentials, they weren't as good as the equivalent mainstream product. When I went back to work, I talked to Roger and Brian about it – do you remember them?'

Roger and Brian are the co-founders of Earthkind. I met them a couple of times when I went to Josh's office. They're exactly how you would picture them: long beards, faded clothes, evangelical zeal. I nod to Josh to continue.

'They got pretty excited and suggested I move into the buying team, to see if I could improve the range. It turns out I'm pretty good at it, and now I'm the head buyer.'

'That's amazing, Josh. Well done!'

'Like I said, it's all down to you. Whenever I'm looking at a potential new product, I apply what I call the "Charley test" to it. "What would Charley say about this?" I ask myself. It's worked like a charm. Sales are through the roof, and Roger and Brian are delighted. Take this jacket, for example.' He hands it over for me to inspect. 'We had a vegan leather jacket in the range before, but it was made of polyurethane and it wasn't very convincing. We sold a few, but the only people that bought them were hardcore vegans. This one is made from pineapple leaf fibres, would you believe. Not only does it look and feel like real leather, but we're using a by-product of normal pineapple production, so no extra resources are needed to produce it.'

I have to admit, the jacket is pretty convincing, and there's a quality, premium feel to it.

'We've been selling them faster than we can get them,' Josh continues. 'In fact, I'm flying out to Jamaica in a couple of days to meet a potential new supplier.'

'I'm sorry, I think I misheard,' I say to him. 'Did you say you were *flying*? What about the carbon emissions?'

He has the grace to look bashful. 'It's not ideal,' he admits, 'but we had a major issue with a fabric supplier earlier this year. We thought we were dealing with an ethical company that was producing clothes made from recycled products, until we were contacted by a national newspaper who painted a very different picture. It was a tricky time, as I'm sure you can imagine. Our premium, eco-friendly garments were actually being made in a sweat shop from ordinary cotton. We dropped the range immediately, the paper was very understanding and published the article reasonably sympathetically, but we nearly got badly burned. Ever since then, there's been a company rule that we have to deal with every new supplier face to face and make sure that they are who they say they are. We try to carbon offset every trip, but it turns out that even a company like ours can't do without fossil fuels completely.'

As the evening wears on, my hostility to him fades away. I can't help it – he's Josh after all, and he knows me probably better than anyone apart from my parents. He's still funny, self-deprecating and all the things I always liked about him. He asks about my life, and I tell him about the flat and a few stories about work. I mention the holiday, but I don't tell him about Ed. Somehow, sharing that I've had another failed relationship feels as if it would be playing into his hands. At the moment, I have the complete moral high ground, and I'm not willing to give that up. It's irrational, I know. I have nothing to be ashamed of where Ed is concerned, but I still don't want Josh to know about him.

We emerge from the pub into the pouring rain. 'Did you walk here?' I ask him.

'Yes, don't worry though. It's a good test for the jacket.' He smiles.

'Don't be silly, I'll give you a lift. Come on.'

I can see his surprise when I press the button and the indicators on the Fiesta flash.

'Nice car,' he says once he's climbed in. 'It's a bit of a step up from the Micra. What did you do with all the tapes?'

'I binned them.'

He puts his hands to his cheeks in mock horror. 'What, even *Now That's What I Call Music*? That was going to make my fortune!'

''Fraid so.'

I drive him to his flat and park outside.

'Charley,' he says, 'I promise I'm not being creepy or anything, but would you like to come in for a coffee? I'd appreciate your opinion on something.'

'I don't know, Josh.'

He looks disappointed. I have enjoyed his company this evening, and it's not late, so I relent.

'OK, why not? But only coffee.'

'Fine.'

Mads is away doing some piece about chic places to stay in Mallorca, but I can still hear her voice shouting, *What the hell are you doing?* as I climb the stairs. *Relax, it's only coffee. I can handle myself*, I reply silently.

The flat is exactly as it was when I left. Well, not quite. Something is different, and it takes me a while to work out what it is. It's immaculately tidy. When I lived here there were always little bits of mess – a magazine left open on the coffee table, or a mug that hadn't quite made it to the dishwasher. But now it's spotless and everything is in its place.

I sit down in my usual place on the sofa, while Josh busies himself making the coffee; apparently, it's a new brand they're trialling. After a couple of minutes, he comes over with two steaming mugs, which he places down on the table before sitting down next to me.

'It's very tidy in here. Are you some sort of neat freak now?' I ask him.

He smiles. 'After Scarlett I just felt I needed to get some control back, you know? I guess tidying the place up, and keeping it tidy, is my way of doing that.'

I sip my coffee. It's delicious, and I tell him so.

'I've really missed you,' Josh says.

'I've missed you too,' I say. In this moment I mean it. We'll never be lovers again, but I'm definitely coming around to the idea of friendship. I look into his eyes and smile.

The kiss catches me by surprise. It's familiar and yet totally new, all at once, and I'm not sure how to react. Josh takes my lack of action as encouragement and deepens the kiss. I'm in total paralysis. I don't want him kissing me, but for some reason I'm not pushing him off. I'm very aware of his beard, which is a bit tickly, and his technique is a little clumsy when I compare it to Ed's. But I still don't move. I don't reject him, and I can't for the life of me work out why. He doesn't seem to notice that I'm not kissing him back.

Even though it's only been a few seconds since his lips first touched mine, he's obviously a man in a hurry. His hand is already on my breast, and he wastes no time in lifting my top, moving it under the fabric of my bra and starting to tweak my nipple. His other hand moves to my crotch. And that's when I come to my senses.

This is horrible. His tongue is flopping around in my mouth, his beard is scratchy, and I can feel my skin already reddening underneath it. I have no idea what he's attempting to do with my nipple, but I'm tempted to tell him that he'll get the rinse and spin cycle if he turns the other way. The fingers of the hand he has on my crotch are stroking me through my jeans, but in my unaroused state the whole experience is chafe-y and unpleasant.

'No,' I say to him as I pull away and stand up, adjusting my bra so it's back in the correct position. 'I don't want this. I think I should go now.'

He looks mortified. 'I'm sorry. It was a crass thing to do. It's just that we've been getting on so well, and you look so amazing, I couldn't help myself. Please stay and finish your coffee at least. I'll behave, I promise,' he says.

'I don't think that's a good idea. Look, it was nice to see you this evening. I'm glad work is going well for you, but there's never going to be anything between you and me. Goodnight, Josh.'

I stand up and walk out of the flat, closing the door softly behind me. By the time I reach the main door of the apartment block, I've already unfriended him and blocked him. As I drive away, I spot his silhouette in the window, watching me. His shoulders are slumped in defeat, but I feel no sympathy for him at all.

25

It's the first episode of *Married Before We Met* tonight. Mum and Dad are eager to watch it, so Mads is picking me up and then we're going to have something to eat with my parents and all watch it together. She was typically robust when I told her what had happened with Josh, and berated me for even considering going up to the flat.

As I'm leaving the surgery, Rachel is gathering her stuff together.

'Any plans for the evening?' I ask her.

'Going out with a few friends. Nothing special. You?'

'Oh, no plans. Quiet night in, I reckon.'

Breathing a sigh of relief that it doesn't sound like she watches the show, I head out to the car park and drive home.

Mads arrives early and is practically bouncing off the walls with excitement.

'I'm finally going to see Ed the bastard in the flesh!' she enthuses. 'I'm going to be flicking V signs at him whenever he's on screen, so be prepared.'

'You've already seen him on LinkedIn, remember? And I'm still not convinced he's a bastard.'

'That was only a tiny picture. I'm going to see him properly now, hear his voice and pick up his mannerisms. I need to understand what you saw in him. How do you feel about seeing him again?'

I'm not really sure how I feel. I still think about him, of course, and sometimes I wonder how things might have been different if my phone hadn't ended up in the ice bucket and I'd managed to speak to him directly. Would he have answered? Would he have had the guts to tell me to my face that he didn't want to see me, rather than hiding behind his PA? Mads and I do at least agree that it was pretty cowardly of him to get her to do the dirty work, much as I don't like her, but the raw ache of missing him has subsided.

Mads' enthusiasm is infectious, however, and by the time we sit down to watch the programme, she's carried my parents along with her.

'I liked him,' my mother tells her, wistfully. 'He and Charlotte made a lovely couple. Such a pity that he turned out the way he did. He seemed so genuine.'

The credits roll, the voice over explains the concept, and there's a montage of the selection process. This year's experts are a psychologist, a relationship counsellor, and a neuro-psychotherapist, whatever one of those is. The first couple to be matched are John and Daisy. He's a farmer from the West Country and she's a showjumper.

'Good match,' Mads declares. 'Both outdoorsy, country people.'

'I'm not so sure,' I opine. 'Physically they're very different.

He's huge, and she's a tiny thing. He could probably crush her with one hand.'

'As long as she goes on top, they'll be fine!' she replies, causing my mother's eyebrows to shoot up.

'They don't show us... you know?' she asks.

Mads bursts out laughing. 'Relax, Christine. I know it's Channel 4 but there won't be any funny business, I promise.'

The next couple is Ed and Sarah. Even after all this time, my heart lurches when I see him, but I try not to give anything away. Mads will spot even the tiniest sign of weakness. Sarah is very pretty; she's also an entrepreneur with her own cosmetics company.

'Well, that's a stupid match straight away!' I exclaim.

Mads raises her eyebrows and studies me for a moment. I can feel her eyes boring into mine, as if she's trying to read my mind. 'You seem to feel surprisingly strongly about this, Charley,' she observes, eventually. 'Would you like to share your reasoning with the room?'

So much for my poker face. I might as well have stood up and announced that I still feel something for him.

'He's a lawyer working long hours,' I explain, desperately trying to cover my tracks. 'She's got her own company so is bound to work all the hours she can. They're never going to see each other.'

Sure enough, one of the criteria they're matched on is their strong work ethic. I throw my hands up in despair.

The final couple is Brian and Rosa. They're older and have both been married before. He has two teenage children, and she has a grown-up son. She tells the camera that she has her heart set on marrying an Italian, because she loves the language, so we agree she's going to be disappointed when she finds out he's from Bolton. They're matched because... well, we can't actually work out why they have been matched beyond the fact that they've both been married before and have children.

I can feel Mads watching me as I follow Ed's progress. This is as close as I'm ever going to get to meeting his friends and family, so I drink them in. His friends seem really nice and, although they're surprised when he tells them what he's doing, they rally round him. Michael, his best man, is a friend from university and is also a lawyer. Ed's pieces to camera about why he's signed up for the experiment and what he's looking for come across as genuine and, try as I might, I just can't reconcile this Ed with the one that ghosted me through his PA. Even Mads has stopped making obscene gestures and is listening closely.

His mum is difficult to read, but his dad reacts particularly badly to the news that he's going to marry someone he's never met, and initially threatens to have him sectioned. His sister, Lily, is lovely. I'm sure we'd have been great friends if Ed and I had made it.

Normally, when I watch this show with Mads, I follow all the couples with the same amount of interest, but this time I'm struggling to care about John and Daisy or Brian and Rosa. I just want to watch Ed and Sarah. I'm fascinated by her. This is the woman that Ed could have married. She doesn't seem his type at all, or at least what I imagine his type to be. She's high maintenance and demanding. Her friends make lots of jokes about how badly she reacts when things don't go her way, and sure enough there is a spectacular meltdown over her wedding dress when she finds out that it's way more expensive than the budget set by the programme and her father is refusing to fund the shortfall. She's obviously been Daddy's little princess all her life, and she's totally unprepared for the strength of his reaction when she announces what she's signed up to. After endless tantrums, the poor guy is worn down and relents.

'What a spoilt little cow!' Mads observes.

I try to give some attention to the other couples. John is very quietly spoken and seems easily overwhelmed by the process of getting married. He's like a rabbit in the headlights in the suit shop, and fidgets uncomfortably in his shirt and tie. Daisy reminds me a bit of Mads; she's very direct and level-headed. If I had to put money on one of these couples, I'd put it on them. She'll be a good foil for him as long as she doesn't overpower him.

Brian and Rosa haven't even met, but they're already like a slow-motion car crash. She's totally unrealistic and keeps going on about Italian men being passionate lovers, and Italian being the language of love. He, on the other hand, owns a second-hand car business, and his idea of fun is an evening out with his mates.

'What were they thinking?' I murmur, and the others agree.

John and Daisy's wedding is shown first. He's bright red in the face and looks incredibly uncomfortable in his suit. He's biting his lip with nerves and my heart goes out to him. 'It'll be OK, mate,' I mouth at him. Daisy looks stunning in a very plain, off-the-shoulder cream dress that hugs her slender torso and swishes along the carpet as she walks. If she's nervous she doesn't show it, and she says her vows clearly and without hesitation. Poor John, on the other hand, stumbles through his, and seems to be getting redder and redder as the ceremony progresses. He's starting to resemble a beetroot.

At last the screen goes up and they see each other. His delight is plain, as his face erupts in an enormous smile. Her reaction is a little harder to judge, but she doesn't seem overtly disappointed. They exchange rings and she lets him give her a tiny kiss on the lips. In the pieces to camera after they've had a chance to introduce themselves to each other and done the photos, she admits that he isn't what she'd imagined, but he seems really nice and she can see why the experts had thought they might be a good match. He, on the other hand, is over the moon and keeps saying how beautiful she is.

Their reception is a good-natured affair, and they seem to be getting on well. There are whispered conversations and a few more shy kisses. His speech is short and heartfelt, but it seems to hit the right note, as she gives him a smacker when he sits down. The friends and family seem to think they're a good match, and point out that there's been lots of eye contact and physical closeness. It's fair to say that the first dance is a disaster, though. Poor John does his best and shuffles around manfully, but we're all relieved when the other guests join in to take the spotlight off him. When they get to the hotel room, he carries her across the threshold and we leave them there.

Next up are Brian and Rosa. Brian's suit looks a little cheap and ill-fitting to me, and he's obviously nervous because he's sweating buckets. It's literally running down his face, and I feel terribly sorry for him. Rosa arrives in a peach-coloured dress that makes her look like one of those knitted dolls people have to cover their spare loo rolls. It's truly hideous. As soon as he starts saying his vows you can see her face drop, and she makes no secret of her disappointment when the screen goes up. No kissing on the lips here; she barely lets him kiss her on the cheek. When it comes to the piece to camera her first words are, 'I asked for an Italian! Why didn't they give me an Italian? Have you seen how sweaty he is? I hate sweaty men.' His tone is a little more conciliatory, and he says, 'She's not the sort of person that I would normally go for, but the experts obviously saw something and I'm happy to trust them.'

'FOOL!' Mads yells at the TV, making my father jump. I think he was probably starting to nod off. This really isn't his type of show.

Things don't improve at the reception. Brian is attentive to Rosa, but she's barely civil to him, and there is no further physical contact, even during the first dance. When they get to the hotel, she doesn't even construct the customary pillow barrier down the centre of the bed that the brides usually do to stop their new husbands getting any ideas; Brian is banished to sleep on the sofa.

'I'll be amazed if they make it to the end of the honeymoon,' I say. Mads nods her agreement.

'They certainly don't seem a very good match,' Mum agrees.

Finally, it's Ed's turn. He looks very smart in his morning coat, and my eyes are glued to him. I'm aware of Mads still watching me, but I don't care any more. It's like we're back in Antigua, somehow, and none of the stuff since has happened. I can almost smell his distinctive aftershave, and I'm caught unaware by my ache of longing for him. The camera cuts to

Sarah and her father in the car. She looks beautiful, and her dress, what I can see of it, has that effortless elegance that only happens when you spend eye-watering amounts of money. Her father is having one last go at talking her out of it and he's very persuasive. He expresses his disappointment that a day which should be the proudest of his life is nothing more than a circus, his concern that Ed won't understand her and will expect her to give up the business she's fought so hard to build, and is basically trying everything he can to ram home the sheer irresponsibility of what she's doing.

The editors, typically, make as much as they can of it all. The footage swaps repeatedly between shots of the car getting closer to the venue, Ed standing waiting for his bride, and the conversation between Sarah and her father. When they finally pull up at the venue, he turns to her and says, 'This is it. This is your last chance. You can get out of this car and commit an act of sheer folly, or you can come to your senses. What's it to be?'

They're really milking it now. The footage cuts repeatedly between her conflicted face and an increasingly agitated Ed, before cutting to an ad break.

'You seemed to be concentrating particularly hard during the last section,' Mads comments as an advert for toothpaste plays out on screen. 'Did you remember to breathe?'

'Didn't he look smart in his morning coat though?' Mum interjects before I have a chance to tell Mads to piss off. 'Quite the dashing gentleman. If I didn't know what he was really like, I'd quite fancy him myself...'

When the ads are finished, the programme restarts back where we left it, with Sarah's decision hanging in the balance. Eventually, she decides that her father is right, and we see the car driving slowly away, cut away with Ed receiving the news that she's not coming.

Ed's piece to camera, from the hotel room he and Sarah should have shared on their wedding night, is far more gracious than I would have managed in the circumstances. Where I would have been ranting, 'How dare she think I'm not good enough!' he is compassionate and forgiving. He does express his disappointment and embarrassment, but doesn't direct any anger at her. The screen moves on to the previews for the next episode, and Mum turns off the TV as the credits start to roll.

I turn to Mads. 'Do you see what I mean about him? It just doesn't add up, does it?'

I hear Mads mutter something under her breath. I can't quite make it out, but it sounds very like 'Oh, for fuck's sake!'

26

Rachel is already there when I get to work on Saturday morning.

'How was your evening out?' I ask her.

'It didn't happen. My friend, Ruth, got let down by her babysitter and Naomi isn't well, so we've postponed it. I ended up staying in and watching *Married Before We Met* on Channel 4. Some poor guy got abandoned at the altar by his bride. Silly cow. I'd have snapped him up, he was gorgeous. It's quite compelling though. You should watch it.'

'I did watch it,' I tell her. 'I don't think Brian and Rosa are going to make it, but I'm hopeful about John and Daisy. I felt sorry for Ed, but I'm not sure she was right for him anyway.'

'No,' Rachel agrees, 'I didn't like her at all and, as for her dad, I wanted to slap him and tell him to butt out!'

I laugh and head to my room to get ready for the morning's patients. I could have done without Rachel watching it. I hope that whatever Ed did to 'sort it' involved the footage of me landing on the cutting room floor, otherwise I'm in for weeks of ribbing from my colleagues when Rachel tells them. I'm not convinced it will, though. If I were pervy Dave, I'd be fighting tooth and nail to keep me in. I'm exactly the sort of car-crash TV that audiences love, especially if they filmed me running away, which I bet they did.

Seeing Ed again, even if it's only on the screen, has knocked me off balance. While I'm preparing my tools for the first patient, I wonder what he's doing now. Maybe he's found someone else and is curled up in bed reading the Saturday papers with her, or maybe they're having noisy weekend sex, before going out for a walk in the park. Thinking about Ed having sex with someone else causes an ache in my chest, and I find myself asking what the girlfriend, who only exists in my imagination, has that I patently didn't.

Thankfully, it's a busy morning and the usual difficult Saturday crowd, so I'm able to forget about Ed's sex life as I concentrate on my work. Seeing him has definitely reopened the wound though, and he keeps crashing into my conscious-ness for the rest of the weekend. I'm back to raking over all the ifs and buts that Mads and I came up with when it was still all fresh, so I'm grateful for the distraction of Sunday lunch with Mum and Dad. Emma, Simon, the girls and Lulu are there too. The girls corner me and talk me to death with stories of school and who their current friends are. I'd forgotten how fickle friendships are at that age. Lulu is a honey-coloured cockapoo, and is absolutely sweet. She seems to sense that all is not quite right in my world and keeps rushing over to me, seeking attention.

I wake up thinking about Ed on Monday morning and tell myself firmly to get a grip. Whatever he's doing now, and whomever he's doing it with, is nothing to do with me any more; he made that perfectly clear when he got his PA to screen my calls. I bury myself in my work during the day and start watching a Scandi-noir box set called *Until the Dawn* in the evening to prevent my mind from wandering back to him. It's typical of the genre; it's always dark, raining, and the body count is racking up while the chain-smoking detective tries to solve the case. The combination of the complexity of the plot and dealing with subtitles requires all my attention.

I'm watching episode five on Wednesday evening when Mads calls. I haven't spoken to her since Friday, as I wasn't sure her unique brand of tough love would have helped me in my current predicament. Wherever she's calling from is noisy, and she's shouting down the phone.

'Hi, I can't talk for long as I'm out with a friend,' she yells. 'He's just gone to the bar to get drinks, so I've got a couple of minutes, tops. Listen, are you OK to drive yourself to your mum and dad's this Friday? I've got a work thing on, so I'll come straight from the station and meet you there.'

'Sure, no problem. Who's the friend?'

'Nobody you'd know. I'll see you on Friday, yeah?'

Probably another Tinder date, I think as she rings off.

On Friday evening, Mads' car is already there when I arrive at Mum and Dad's. I'm a bit apprehensive as it's the honeymoon episode tonight, so if I'm going to feature it will be in this one. I'm also a bit worried that another dose of Ed on TV is going to undo all the work I've done this week to try to regain my equilibrium.

I call out a hello as I let myself in through the front door, but nobody replies. I can hear voices coming from the kitchen though, so I head that way. As I push open the door, I see Mum, Dad and Mads with glasses in their hands. They aren't alone though. There's another person in the kitchen.

Standing just behind Mads, looking straight at me, is Ed.

I'm very glad I'm not holding anything, as I would certainly drop it. I'm sure my mouth drops open.

'Ah, there you are, love!' My mother comes and gives me a hug. 'Look who's here!'

I seem to be having trouble speaking. I manage a strangled-sounding 'Hi, Ed.'

'Hi, Charley,' he replies. He looks every bit as uncomfortable as me.

'Umm, Mads. Can I borrow you for a minute?' I say, before dragging her out of the kitchen and into the sitting room. I'm conscious of an uneasy silence behind me, but I might be about to murder my best friend and I don't want an audience.

'What the fuck have you done? Talk!' I hiss at her as soon as we're in the sitting room.

As usual, she's totally unfazed by my ferocity.

'You're still in love with him,' she says, simply. 'You may not know it, but you are. The Ed shrine that is your flat is a pretty big clue, but watching you watching him last week was the final confirmation. I realised that you were never going to move on unless we got to the bottom of what happened, so I staged an intervention.'

'Oh, God. What did you do?'

She smiles. 'Well, first I think we need to give me credit for having the lady-balls to find Ed and get him to come here. You're finally going to get your answers because of me.'

'Fine. You've got the biggest lady-balls in the world. Now,

what did you *do*?' I just manage to avoid adding, 'And who do I have to apologise to?'

'It was rather brilliant, even if I say so myself,' she continues, totally unaffected by the meltdown going on in front of her. 'The problem, as I saw it, was how to bypass Miss Frosty-Tits, the PA. The most obvious thing was simply to call and make an appointment. I did a bit of internet research and, even though their website didn't mention fees at all, most of the other divorce lawyer sites offered a free initial consultation. So I worked out a cover story, called up and fed it to the PA.'

'What happened?' Despite my irritation with her, I can't help but be intrigued.

'She told me that the earliest appointment she could offer me was three weeks away, which took the wind out of my sails a bit. There was no way I could put up with you mooning at the screen for another three weeks. She also told me, get this, the initial consultation attracts a "discounted rate" of four hundred pounds for the hour, with an extra two hundred and fifty if I wanted the "discretion of entering via the under-ground garage". I love you to bits, but there's no way I could afford that. Who charges four hundred pounds an hour and calls it a discount? Anyway, luckily for you, I'm a quick thinker. If I couldn't afford an appointment with him, I worked out that I still had the option to catch him either on his way into the building or on his way out. You'd already told me he works late a lot, so that kind of ruled out catching him on the way out, as I don't think hanging around offices late at night is a good thing for a woman on her own to be doing. It had to be done as he arrived. But what time does someone like Ed start work?

'I told Frosty-Tits that three weeks and the fee was fine, as long as the meeting was first thing in the morning. I then asked her what the earliest time was that he could see me. Thinking that I was now a serious prospect, she was putty in my hands. She told me that he normally started at eight thirty but could meet at eight if I was able to give sufficient notice.'

'But didn't you still have to book the appointment and pay?'

'No. I pretended someone was at the door, told her I'd call back with my credit card number in a few minutes and hung up. Then, on Wednesday, I rocked up at the building reception just after eight in the morning. I told the security guard that I was waiting for a colleague, to make sure he left me alone. I recognised Ed from your shrine as soon as he walked in and intercepted him. I explained who I was and that I needed to talk to him about you. He told me he had an early meeting so we couldn't talk there and then, but he suggested we meet in a pub near his office that evening. I thought he was probably just trying to get rid of me so, before he managed to escape through the barriers, I gave him a piece of my mind about the way he ghosted you and told him I didn't believe he'd turn up and face me after being such a coward. I wasn't going to let him get away with that.'

'What happened?'

'It stopped him in his tracks. He said that if anyone was guilty of ghosting, it was you. He was pretty riled and we ended up having a bit of a row. It was weird, because we were both furious but also whispering so other people couldn't overhear.'

'How can he possibly think I ghosted him?' I exclaim. 'I

tried every bloody thing I could think of, and he refused to take my calls!'

'And now we get to the heart of it. Here's the bit you need to hear, OK? He swears blind that his PA never passed on your message, he never got your letter, and he certainly never told her to screen your call.'

'Do you believe him?'

'I do, yes.'

'But why would she do that?'

'That's a good question that he couldn't answer there and then, and we were running out of time as it turned out he really did have a meeting, but he promised that he would turn up at the pub, because he was as eager to get to the bottom of it as I was.'

'And did he?'

'Yes. He told me he'd asked his PA about it and she'd pretended not to remember. He called her out on it, so you can assume she's seriously in the shit. I'll let him fill you in on the details, but the point is that he was gutted that you thought he'd ghosted you. He said he was really looking forward to hearing from you after he left his number but, when you never called...'

'Did you tell him about my phone?'

'Yes. Why do you think he's here? Once we'd ironed out what had really happened and worked out that neither of you had done what the other thought, I came up with the idea of him coming tonight as a surprise, so you could clear the air properly. I spoke to your mum, who understandably wasn't keen to begin with, but she came round as soon as I told her the real story. Then I collected him from the station on my way here, and ta-dah! You can thank me now.'

'Hang on a minute. So when you called me on Wednesday, you were with Ed?'

'Yes. We'd just concocted the plan, but he needed collecting from the station, which is why I couldn't pick you up. It would have spoiled the surprise.'

'Honestly, Mads. I don't know whether to hug you or kill you.'

'Why don't you see how the evening pans out and decide at the end? Now, shall we go back into the kitchen before he escapes again?'

I feel like I've stepped into some kind of parallel universe as we walk back into the kitchen. Ed is here, in my parents' house, chatting away to Mum and Dad as if the last six months never happened. When he sees me, he tenses, obviously unsure how I feel about him being here. I walk over to him and give him a hug. I get a delicious whiff of his aftershave as I inhale.

'It's nice to see you,' I murmur into his ear.

'It's really nice to see you too. I'm so, so sorry about the mix-up. I don't know what Alice thought she was doing,' he replies. 'I couldn't understand why you didn't call. I kept checking my phone in case I'd put it on silent by mistake.'

'I know all about that,' I reply, wryly. 'It sounds like we have a lot of catching up to do, and a lot of misconceptions to unravel.'

After dinner, we settle down to watch the episode. Mads, Mum and Dad arrange themselves so that my only option is to share a sofa with Ed. Part of me wants to cuddle into him, but I hold back. Even though the rational part of me wants to believe his story, I'm not quite there yet.

'Tonight, on *Married Before We Met*, our couples head off on honeymoon,' the voiceover tells us. 'There's going to be romance, tears, and a big revelation from Ed!'

I look at him questioningly. I thought he said he'd sorted it?

'It'll be fine,' he whispers.

Most of the programme, as expected, focuses on John and Daisy and Brian and Rosa. John and Daisy are on safari in Botswana and seem to be getting on famously. He's obviously besotted with her, and she's continuing to warm up to him in return. Brian and Rosa are struggling. They're in Barbados and, to cap all his other failings in her eyes, it turns out Brian is a bit of a snorer, so she's banished him to another room. They do manage to find some common ground through the intimacy questionnaire though, as it turns out their previous marriages both broke down due to their spouse's infidelity. Towards the end of the episode they are talking much more openly to each other and even holding hands, so we don't write them off just yet.

The final ad break comes around and I pop to the loo. I need a moment to prepare myself for what's coming. I come back in just as the final segment of the episode is starting.

'Last week Ed was left standing at the altar,' the voiceover is saying. 'We join him on his own in Antigua, to see how he's getting on.' A montage of shots of Ed follows. There's Ed walking around the resort, Ed lying on a sunbed reading, Ed eating on his balcony and then we cut to the interview. My hands start sweating as I relive that morning. There he is, speaking to the camera from the sofa in the honeymoon suite, while I'm hiding just through the wall behind him in the bedroom. I remember all the questions, and his answers.

'And how do you feel about the future now?' pervy Dave's voice asks from behind the camera. His accent is more upmarket in professional mode, and he sounds like he genuinely cares, but I'm not fooled. I don't remember this part of the interview though, and I frown slightly.

'Optimistic,' Ed replies. 'I've met someone special, actually.'

'On your honeymoon? How exciting!' pervy Dave says. 'Do you think she might be the one?'

'It's too early to say for sure, but let's say that she might be, yes.'

My mouth drops open again and I turn to look at Ed. He's studiously avoiding my gaze by staring fixedly at the TV.

On the screen, Ed is telling pervy Dave about how we met and how wonderful I am, and I suddenly feel like an awful human being. Here he is, saying all this amazing stuff about me, while I was trying to get as far away from him as I could. I didn't deserve him, I realise, and a tear slips down my cheek, followed closely by another. Thankfully, everyone else is glued to the TV and nobody notices. I wipe them away surreptitiously.

The closing credits roll, and I realise with relief that Ed has been as good as his word. None of the footage of me was included.

'How did you do it?' I ask him.

'Actually, it was a lot easier than you might think,' he replies. 'I told Dave he couldn't use the footage he took of you because, although I was under contract, you weren't. He came back at me and said he could film whatever he wanted in a public space, so I told him a hotel room didn't count as public. He got really pissed off and started demanding I go and find you and get you to sign a consent form or the production company would sue me for breach of contract, so I hit him with a load of legal mumbo-jumbo about coercion and so on, and eventually we compromised. I agreed that I'd do an extra bit of the interview about meeting you in return for him leaving you alone. I came to find you afterwards, to tell you what I'd done, but you'd gone.'

'I'm so sorry. I panicked,' I tell him.

'It was my fault. I should have remembered they were coming,' he replies.

'Charley,' Mads pipes up suddenly, 'I have an early start in the morning so I'm going to head off. Are you OK to drop Ed back at the station on your way home?'

She's unbelievable. I follow her into the hallway to see her off.

'My work here is done,' she tells me. 'Don't fuck it up again, will you?'

27

I'm very conscious of Ed's presence in my car as we drive to the station. His aftershave hangs in the confined space as he sits with his hands on his lap, looking straight ahead through the windscreen. It's only a few minutes' drive and we travel in silence. When we get to the station, I pull into the car park and switch off the engine. Ed undoes his seat belt but doesn't get out of the car.

'Charley, I'm really sorry about Alice. She was completely out of order. I have no idea what she thought she was doing. She must have known who you were, because I'd told her about you when she asked how *Married Before We Met* was going.'

'So why did she tell me you didn't want to speak to me? Why did she tell me to stop calling?'

'When Mads confronted me in the lobby, my first instinct was to not believe her. Alice has always been a hundred per cent trustworthy. But Mads was so fierce about it that I decided to check. We record all our calls, so I went into the system to listen to the recordings from the days that Mads told me you called and it was all exactly as she described. I was devastated and furious in equal measure. I called Alice into my office and played the recordings to her.'

'What did she say?'

'She said she thought you were a journalist. We get quite a lot of calls where journalists pretend to be friends or family, just to get through and try to get the inside story on some of our cases. I don't know what they think they're going to achieve, as there's no way we would ever tell them anything. But even still, the protocol is that, if she's suspicious, she's supposed to say I'm busy, take the number and pass it on to me, just in case it's a genuine call and I recognise the person.'

'But she didn't do it with my number?'

'No. I asked her about it and she said she must have mislaid it. Then, when you called again and I hadn't added you to the trusted numbers list, she decided you were a nuisance caller and told you not to call again.'

'That's pretty unprofessional, isn't it, to mislay someone's contact details? What if I'd been somebody important?'

'You *are* somebody important!' he exclaims. 'I'm still furious with her and I've threatened to raise it with HR as a disciplinary issue. Believe me, she knows she's done the wrong thing.'

'Will you?'

'Probably not. I'd like to, but the company has policies on taking personal calls on the office line, so I'd probably get a bit of flak too because I'd have to explain who you are. But she doesn't know that, so I'm letting her stew for the time being.'

'Do you remember when you first told me about her, you said she was really anti you being on the show?'

'What about it?'

'You don't think she's got designs on you, do you?'

'I'm sure she hasn't,' he replies, with complete certainty. 'It would be unprofessional and, besides, we've worked together for years; something would have leaked out by now.'

'Mm. I'm not convinced, if you don't mind me saying. However, you know her better than me, so I'll leave that one with you.'

Silence falls. He's staring straight ahead out of the windscreen and his face is unreadable. My guess is that he's contemplating what I've said and trying to marry it up to his own experience. By the look of him, it's not going that well. I feel slightly uncomfortable and I'm starting to wish I'd never said anything about it.

'I'm really glad you came tonight,' I say, to break the silence. 'I was so confused and hurt when you gave me your number and then wouldn't take my call. It's nice to know what really happened, even if we don't agree on the motive.'

He turns back to face me and his expression clears. 'I'm really pleased I came too,' he replies. 'When I didn't hear from you, I assumed that you didn't want to contact me. I did find you on the internet and thought about messaging you, but in the end I decided to do the gentlemanly thing and not make a nuisance of myself. If I'd known that you'd called I would have called you back straight away.'

'I wrote to you as well,' I say to him.

'Mads told me. Honestly, I never got the letter. It must have gone astray somewhere.'

I roll my eyes. It's very clear to me now where it went astray, but I'm not going to push Ed any more about his PA's obvious crush on him; I get the impression he's not ready to hear it and I don't really want to talk about her any more either.

'I'm sorry about Mads,' I tell him. 'I hope she didn't make things awkward for you at work.'

He laughs. 'You were right about her, she is a force of nature. When she accosted me in the lobby of the office on Wednesday morning, I worked out who she was as soon as she told me her name. She's not someone to be on the wrong side of, that's for sure. Thankfully, she softened a bit when we worked out what had happened. She even told me a bit about how you'd been. Tell me, do you really have a shrine to me in your flat?'

I'm going to kill her. Thankfully it's dark, so he can't see the blazing embarrassment on my cheeks.

'It's not a shrine!' I say, more forcefully than I intend. 'It's just a collection of photos from the holiday, some of which happen to have you in them.'

A London-bound train rolls into the station. Neither of us moves and the train leaves. We continue to sit, talking. He tells me about the steps he's taken to improve his work–life balance, and I fill him in on my life since I saw him last, such as it is. He's suitably impressed when I tell him about the water-skiing and windsurfing lessons, and we reminisce about the activities we did together. Neither of us mentions the sex, although it hangs unspoken between us. Trains come and go.

'So, is there anyone special in your life?' I ask him, as yet another London-bound train departs. 'Did Sarah realise her mistake and come crawling back, begging for forgiveness?'

'No, and no,' he replies. 'Michael, who was my best man, persuaded me to sign up to Tinder a month or so ago. I've been on a couple of dates, but they didn't come to anything.'

'Why not?' I ask. I'm trying to keep my voice steady, but the fact that he's single has caused something strange to surge through me, and I'm feeling a bit trembly.

'Don't get me wrong, they were both lovely people, and attractive. But... umm... I'm not sure I should tell you this...'

'Go on,' I urge. 'What was wrong with them?'

He looks at me, and his eyes glitter in the darkness. 'They weren't you,' he says, simply.

I can't believe what he just said. It's like the last six months are falling away, and we're having the reunion we should have had as soon as I got back from Antigua.

'What about you?' he asks.

I don't want to tell him, but I know it wouldn't be fair not to.

'I had a close shave with Josh,' I say. 'I met him for a drink, we got on really well, and then he came on to me. Stupid of me really, I fell for the "come up for coffee" line. I think I was a bit muddled because we'd had such a good evening. Anyway, as soon as he started trying it on, I came to my senses and left.'

'Why didn't you take him back, if you got on so well? You've got a lot of shared history and he's probably learned his lesson.'

'Simple,' I tell him with a smile. 'He wasn't you.'

We sit there in silence for a while, digesting these revelations. Another train rolls into the station and leaves. Ed's hand finds mine in the darkness and the last fragments of doubt fall away as we lean towards each other and our lips meet. It just feels right, and I know for certain that he's my Ed and I never want to let him go again.

Suddenly, the station lights start to go out.

'Shit, Ed, I think you've missed the last train!' I exclaim, breaking off the kiss. I can't help giggling. Here we are, snogging in a car like teenagers.

'Ah. Yes, it does look that way,' he agrees, as the lights continue to go out.

'What are we going to do?'

'There must be a hotel somewhere nearby I can check into. It's not a big deal.' He fishes out his phone and starts searching the internet.

The prospect of driving him to a hotel and leaving him is more than I can bear. I've only just got him back.

'Ed?' I ask.

'Yes?'

'Umm, you could stay with me, if you like?' The words seem to come out before I've even had a chance to think about what I'm saying.

He turns to me and cups my face in his hands. As our mouths meet again, fireworks erupt throughout my body. When we finally break apart, he fastens his seat belt, I start the engine and turn right out of the car park, towards Tonbridge.

EPILOGUE

THE MALDIVES – 18 MONTHS LATER

I'm lying on a sunbed, reading my book, when I sense a shadow falling across me.

'Mrs Wells, I presume?' Ed's voice says.

I glance at the ring on my left hand, sparkling in the sun, and then up at Ed.

'That's me,' I reply.

* * *

Ed ended up staying the whole weekend with me after Mads brought him back into my life that Friday evening. From that point on we spent all the time we could together, either at my flat or in his very swanky bachelor pad in London. After six months, he proposed, and of course I said yes. We explored various places to live, and eventually settled on Sevenoaks, as it's close to London for Ed, and not too bad a commute for me either. Ed sold his flat for an exorbitant sum and we were able to buy our house, which is close enough to the station that Ed can walk there. Mum and Dad like having us close by, but are very careful about not overcrowding us.

Ed's PA never warmed to me, and she never admitted to throwing away my letter or deliberately mislaying my message. It was obvious to me, the first time I met her, that she was madly in love with him, but he couldn't see it and we had quite a heated debate, which I would have lost had she not subsequently confirmed my suspicions by resigning the day after Ed and I announced our engagement. His new PA, Rosie, is lovely and, on the rare occasions I need to ring him at work, I usually end up talking to her for longer than I do him.

My hopes for a simple wedding were dashed by Mum and Mads, who turned full bridezilla on me. It was a beautiful day, though. Ed looked amazing (again) in his morning coat, and there were lots of humorous references in the speeches to the fact that I was the bride who actually turned up.

* * *

Ed flops down on the sunbed next to mine.

'I've booked all the water sports,' he tells me. 'I've spread them out a bit, so we don't overload ourselves like we did in Antigua.'

I smile and lean across to kiss him.

'I've been thinking,' I tell him. 'And I've decided that, as nice as your and Sarah's honeymoon was, I prefer this one.'

'And why is that?' he asks.

'Well, because this is actually my honeymoon rather than someone else's, I'm married to the most amazing man and, best of all, there's no pervy Dave with his bloody camera!'

He laughs and takes me in his arms. 'I can probably call Dave, if you're missing him.'

'I don't think so,' I reply. 'I have plans for you that would probably make even Dave blush.'

'Really? And what might they be?'

'You'll have to wait and see,' I tell him as I take his hand and we set off towards our room.

ACKNOWLEDGMENTS

I am hugely grateful to everyone who has helped me with this book. First of all, to my best friend and partner in crime, Mandy, who challenged me to stop talking about writing and actually sit down to do it. Without you, this would never have happened, so thank you.

Writing a book is just the first step in a long process, and I want to say a massive thank you to my editor, Tara, for her never-ending patience and help, and the entire team at Boldwood who do so much to bring a book from a simple manuscript to the finished article. It's truly a privilege to work with you all.

I also want to thank Frances for her beta reading and helpful suggestions, Sally for her hairdressing advice, and Chris for giving me masses of encouragement when I was first starting out.

Casting the net wider I want to acknowledge Endemol Australia, and their series *Married at First Sight Australia*, which forms the basis for my fictional show *Married Before We Met*. I need to thank Google and YouTube for teaching me to water-ski and windsurf during lockdown, and LoveHoney.co.uk for their highly informative videos on different types of vibrator!

I need, of course, to say thank you to my family for being

so supportive while I've been writing this book, and to the dog for patiently listening to me working out plotlines on our morning walks.

Finally, I want to thank Charlotte and Madison for being such enjoyable characters to write.

MORE FROM PHOEBE MACLEOD

We hope you enjoyed reading *Someone Else's Honeymoon*. If you did, please leave a review.

If you'd like to gift a copy, this book is also available as an ebook, digital audio download and audiobook CD.

Sign up to Phoebe MacLeod's mailing list for news, competitions and updates on future books.

https://bit.ly/PhoebeMacLeodNews

ABOUT THE AUTHOR

Phoebe MacLeod is the author of several popular romantic comedies. She lives in Kent with her partner, grown up children and disobedient dog. Her love for her home county is apparent in her books, which have either been set in Kent or have a Kentish connection. She currently works as an IT consultant and writes in her spare time. She has always had a passion for learning new skills, including cookery courses, learning to drive an HGV and, most recently, qualifying to instruct on a Boeing 737 flight simulator.

Follow Phoebe on social media:

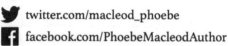

twitter.com/macleod_phoebe
facebook.com/PhoebeMacleodAuthor
instagram.com/phoebemacleod21

Boldwood

Boldwood Books is an award-winning fiction publishing company seeking out the best stories from around the world.

Find out more at www.boldwoodbooks.com

Join our reader community for brilliant books, competitions and offers!

Follow us
@BoldwoodBooks
@BookandTonic

Sign up to our weekly deals newsletter

https://bit.ly/BoldwoodBNewsletter

9 781804 262443